Beethoven's 2nd

The passageway got narrower, and Ted and Emily had to crawl the last few feet between the heating ducts until they found themselves in a tiny space lit by a single dim light-bulb that hung from the dusty ceiling.

It took a moment for Ted and Emily's eyes to get used to the faint light, but when they did, they had the surprise of their lives. There, in the farthest corner of the little space were four tiny St Bernard puppies. The little dogs were trying to crawl and open their tiny eyes, but they were too weak to make even the tiniest little squeak.

Emily's eyes grew wide. 'Little Beethovens!' she said, amazed and delighted.

Beethoven's 2nd

A novel by Robert Tine

Based on the motion picture written by Len Blum

Characters created by Edmond Dantes
and Amy Holden Jones

PUFFIN BOOKS

PUFFIN BOOKS

Published by the Penguin Group
Penguin Books Ltd, 27 Wrights Lane, London W8 5TZ, England
Penguin Books USA Inc., 375 Hudson Street, New York, New York 10014, USA
Penguin Books Australia Ltd, Ringwood, Victoria, Australia
Penguin Books Canada Ltd, 10 Alcorn Avenue, Toronto, Ontario, Canada M4V 3B2
Penguin Books (NZ) Ltd, 182–190 Wairau Road, Auckland 10, New Zealand

Penguin Books Ltd, Registered Offices: Harmondsworth, Middlesex, England

First published in the United States by Putnam Books 1993
Published in Puffin Books 1993
3 5 7 9 10 8 6 4

Puffin Film and TV Tie-in edition first published 1993

Copyright © by MCA Publishing Rights, a division of MCA Inc., 1993
All rights reserved

Typeset by Datix International Limited, Bungay, Suffolk
Filmset in Monophoto Garamond
Printed in England by Clays Ltd, St Ives plc

Chapter 1

He's big . . . He's bad . . . He's Beethoven.

And he's hungry!

Beethoven's big brown wet nose twitched and quivered as the smell of something delicious wafted up the stairs from the Newtons' kitchen. The huge brown-and-white St. Bernard immediately jumped to his feet and thundered down the stairs, his nose to the floor, following the mouth-watering aroma.

In the kitchen Beethoven found all the Newtons gathered at the dining table. There was the littlest Newton, six-year-old Emily and next to her, Ted, her ten-year-old brother. Ryce, the oldest child, sat next to Mrs Newton — and at the head of the table was Beethoven's special favourite, Mr Newton.

The whole family was laughing happily as they sat down to dinner. Emily cut a piece of juicy steak and offered it to her canine friend.

'Here, Beethoven,' she said. Her father looked on, beaming with delight at the gesture.

Beethoven's big, thick, pink tongue slipped out of his mouth and licked the tender morsel off the fork. He swallowed it quickly, and that little juicy titbit only made Beethoven realize just how hungry he really was!

And it was a good thing Beethoven was hungry

because Mrs Newton had a surprise for him. She lifted a silver cover off a big serving tray and placed it under his nose. The platter was stacked high with thick slices of juicy, steaming, rare roast beef.

'Beethoven,' said Mrs Newton, 'this is a little gift from all of us.'

Beethoven could hardly believe his eyes, and he blinked a couple of times in amazement.

Beethoven opened his mouth wide and was about to dig into the roast beef when Mr Newton jumped to his feet. 'Beethoven! No!' he shouted.

Beethoven looked nervously at Mr Newton. Beethoven knew that, deep down, Mr Newton loved him with all his heart – but he also knew that George Newton had very strict rules against spoiling dogs. Beethoven sighed heavily. He knew that the big platter of roast beef was just too good to be true . . .

But he was in for a big surprise.

'We want you to have this!' Mr Newton picked up another covered dish and put it down next to the roast beef. On this plate was a giant bone – it looked so big it must have come from a dinosaur! – and suddenly Beethoven couldn't make up his mind which treat to eat first.

Beethoven licked his lips and his tail thumped on the floor like a bass drum. His big heart flooded with the love he felt for all the Newtons and George Newton in particular.

Then Mr Newton said something that made him even happier. 'And later on, Beethoven, we'll go out in the garden and throw your ball around – just the two of us!'

Beethoven sighed happily and started to eat . . . but somehow he couldn't quite seem to get his teeth into the scrumptious roast beef . . .

Emily and Ted, wearing their pyjamas, sat on the floor and watched as Beethoven slept, snoring slightly, lost in dreamland, absorbed in his fantasy of big meaty bones and juicy roast beef. It had been a long time since Beethoven had come to live with them, but they still thought he was the most interesting thing in their lives. They couldn't take their eyes off him. They were late getting ready for school, but they couldn't tear themselves away.

'What do you suppose dogs dream about?' Emily asked her brother.

Ted took a good hard look at the sleeping dog. Beethoven was sighing heavily in his sleep, and his big pink tongue hung out of his mouth. The look on his face was one of pure happiness.

'I don't know,' Ted said. 'But it must be really good.'

'Yeah,' agreed Emily.

Suddenly, from downstairs Mrs Newton called out. 'Ted! Emily! Are you kids dressed? You'd better hurry up!'

Ted and Emily jumped as if they had received an electric shock.

'Almost ready,' Ted shouted.

'Yeah, Mom, almost!'

The kids scurried for their bedrooms, just as their big sister, Ryce, emerged from the bathroom that the three children shared. The pretty fifteen-year-old girl paused at the top of the staircase.

'Mom!' she shouted down the stairs. 'We're out of toilet paper!'

'OK!' Mrs Newton yelled back. 'Here!'

A second or two later, a roll of soft white toilet paper, thrown by Mrs Newton, sailed up the staircase and bopped Beethoven right on the nose. He awoke in the middle of a snore and looked around him. There was no giant bone, no huge platter of roast beef – it had all been a dream!

But that wasn't so bad. Suddenly he realized that it was a bright new day and he was right in the middle of his wonderful family.

Beethoven jumped to his feet and barked happily. Then he started down the stairs to see what adventures were in store. But before he went out into the big wide world, he knew what he had to do first. He had to get something to eat – because he really was very, very hungry!

Chapter 2

Mr Newton was just sitting down to breakfast. He was dressed in his best suit, ready to go to work. He was talking to his wife about his favourite subject — air fresheners. Mr Newton had started a small business, the Newton Air Freshener Company, and he worked hard there. In fact, next to his family, air fresheners were the most important things in George Newton's life. He was so interested in air fresheners that most of the time he didn't even notice that the rest of the world was not. In fact, Mr Newton could get downright boring on the subject — but his wife Alice didn't mind.

She bustled around the kitchen preparing breakfast for her family, half-listening to her husband. She couldn't pay all her attention to him because she had four different breakfasts to prepare — three different cereals for her children and a plate of bacon and eggs for her husband. George didn't mind that she wasn't exactly listening — he sort of liked listening to himself as he talked about his favourite subject.

'. . . I mean,' he said as he poured himself a cup of coffee, 'when *I* was a kid, that little green

air freshener hanging from the mirror of the car
. . . it meant something.'

'Yes, dear,' said Mrs Newton, flipping a couple of slices of bacon in the frying pan.

Beethoven wandered into the room and looked at the two adults. Then he sniffed the air deeply and licked his chops. There were few things in the world Beethoven liked better than bacon! He was ready for breakfast, even if the rest of the family wasn't!

'Those little air fresheners,' George Newton continued, 'They meant security. Stability. Confidence.'

'Right,' agreed Mrs Newton. She cupped her hands around her mouth and yelled up the stairs to Ted, Emily and Ryce. 'Let's move it! One more time late for school and they take away my licence to be a mother.'

Beethoven lumbered over to his huge dog dish which sat in the corner of the kitchen, ready to see what leftovers and goodies Mrs Newton had put there. His heart sank when he saw that there was nothing left in the bowl except for a few scraps of dry dog food left over from his dinner the night before. In all the confusion, Mrs Newton had forgotten that she had to make not four, but *five* breakfasts.

Mr Newton didn't notice Beethoven's pleading

looks. 'You see,' he said, 'I'm going to see that banker this morning, and he has to understand that air fresheners are more than just ... air fresheners. They're a way of life ...' If Beethoven had known how to talk he would have said, 'Never mind that. How about some food?' After his wonderful dream, Beethoven was not in the mood for leftover dog food. He wanted something really delicious.

But Mr Newton didn't notice the disappointed look on Beethoven's face. 'You see, an air freshener is more than just an ordinary *thing*. It's a symbol. Like Superman's cape. Did he really need a cape? No. But to me it was an important symbol.'

Mrs Newton was still bustling about trying to get breakfast ready for her whole family. 'Well,' she said, 'if this bank manager has any imagination at all, he'll understand what you're trying to do.'

'If he had any imagination, he wouldn't *be* a bank manager,' Mr Newton grumbled.

Beethoven decided it was time to get someone to pay some attention to him. Lying under Mr Newton's chair was Beethoven's lime-green tennis ball. Suddenly, he dived for it, throwing himself beneath the chair – and shoving George back to the wall.

'Whaaa!' he yelled, almost tumbling over backwards.

Beethoven snatched the ball with his mouth and playfully tried to push it into Mr Newton's hand. Two little lines of drool slipped from his mouth and almost stained Mr Newton's trousers.

'Hey! Stop that!' Mr Newton was exasperated. 'No – I don't want to play. And I have a very important meeting this morning so, please, no hair, or drool, on my suit.'

Just then, Ted and Emily rushed into the kitchen and sat down at the table.

'Ready!' said Emily.

Alice Newton placed bowls of cereal in front of her children. 'OK,' she said. 'Eat. And don't stop until you have completely finished ... Where's your sister?'

'Upstairs?' suggested Ted.

Mrs Newton shouted upstairs, 'Ryce! Breakfast!' Then she took a plate of fried eggs and bacon from the stove and put it in front of her husband. 'OK. When you see the banker – what's his name?'

'Bickert. Mr Bickert.'

'OK. Tell me what you're going to say to Mr Bickert.'

Beethoven was not much interested in Mr Newton's speech for the bank manager, but the eggs and bacon *fascinated* him.

Mr Newton thought for a moment. 'I'm going to say, "Mr Bickert, a few months ago I woke up and realized something. Something important . . ."'

'Good,' said Mrs Newton. 'Keep going.'

George Newton was really warming to his subject. 'Mr Bickert, I have spent my entire life trying to make people's cars smell like pine trees . . .' He was getting a faraway look in his eyes as he thought about the wonders of air fresheners. He had lost all interest in his breakfast – but Beethoven hadn't forgotten about it for a second!

Beethoven dropped the tennis ball and very quietly reached up to the table and snatched the bacon from Mr Newton's plate. He swallowed it in a second and licked his muzzle. Food at last!

Mr Newton didn't even notice. '"But I've realized that there's a bigger challenge out there in the world of air fresheners."'

Alice Newton frowned. 'Don't say challenge. Bankers get scared of challenge. Say opportunity. It sounds like money. Bankers like that.'

'OK,' Mr Newton continued. '"There's a new opportunity. An opportunity not just to connect air fresheners with a person's car or truck . . . But to connect air fresheners with a person's entire *life*."' For George Newton, it was a thrilling vision.

Beethoven didn't care. He had the ball in his mouth again and tried to nudge it into Ted's hand.

'Not now, boy,' said Ted, snatching his hand away from the wet tennis ball. 'We're late.'

'Please, Beethoven,' said Mrs Newton, pushing him aside. 'We're trying to eat breakfast here.'

Beethoven wished that he could tell her that *he* had exactly the same idea – he wanted breakfast too! But everyone was too busy to notice. Beethoven looked at the family. Mr Newton was still babbling on about air fresheners – not even his wife was listening to him now – and Ted and Emily were busy eating. Mrs Newton was still fussing at the stove.

Beethoven sighed heavily. Everyone was too occupied to pay any attention to him. Slowly, he walked out of the kitchen and towards the stairs – he might as well as see what Ryce was doing. Maybe she would play with him. Or feed him. Or if he was really lucky – both!

Chapter 3

Ryce had other things on her mind.

Although it was early in the morning, the gossip-line among Ryce and her teenage friends was already buzzing.

When Beethoven got to the girl's room, his ball clutched in his mouth, a hopeful look on his face, he found her on the telephone. Ryce looked absolutely amazed at what her friend Michelle was telling her.

'If you're lying,' Ryce said into the phone, 'I'm going to kill you.'

'I swear to God,' said Michelle solemnly. 'I just finished talking to him like five seconds ago . . .'

The 'him' that Michelle was referring to was Taylor Devereaux, by far the coolest boy in Ryce's class — and one that she had had a secret crush on for years.

'Tell me what he said again,' asked Ryce.

'He specifically asked me to find out if you wanted a lift to school this morning,' Michelle repeated.

Ryce couldn't believe her ears. She was so stunned that when Beethoven tried to nudge the ball into her hand, she absently-mindedly pushed the big dog away.

'He's going to give me a lift?'

'Right.'

'Like – in his convertible?'

'No, in the space shuttle. He'll be here any minute. You want us to pick you up next?'

From the bottom of the stairs Ryce heard her mother's voice. She sounded exasperated this time. 'Ryce! Come down now! While you're still young!'

'Michelle, gotta go.'

'Well? What do I tell him?'

'Tell him yes!' Ryce slammed down the phone and raced for the door. Beethoven lumbered after her, his tennis ball still in his mouth.

Ryce thundered down stairs, taking the steps three at a time. Mrs Newton and Mr Newton were waiting at the bottom.

'Mom! Life is amazing! I'm getting a lift to school this morning with Michelle and Taylor Devereaux!'

'Who's Taylor Devereaux?' her father asked.

'A boy!' Ryce yelled over her shoulder.

'A boy,' said George Newton to himself. 'That's nice . . . I think. Anyway, I'm going to see if the paper has come yet.'

He stepped outside and took a deep breath of

the fresh morning air. Beethoven, right at his side, did the same.

Coming down the street towards the Newton house was a paper boy, pedalling his bike and expertly tossing folded newspapers into the front gardens of every home he passed.

'Hey, Mr Newton,' the paperboy shouted, 'it's the last of the ninth, full count – you call the pitch!'

Mr Newton put down his coffee cup, balancing it on the rail of the front porch. He crouched down as if he was a baseball catcher ready to receive the pitch.

'OK, straight down the pipe, Tommy. Nothing but smoke. Give me the best fastball you've got!'

Tommy reared back and fired the newspaper at Mr Newton – and missed. The paper slammed into the coffee cup and splashed the liquid all over Mr Newton's crisp, clean, white shirt and the front of his trousers.

Beethoven was delighted. If George was playing catch with the paperboy, then he must want to play with the tennis ball as well. Gently, he nudged the ball into George's hand.

But Mr Newton didn't have time to play. He dropped the ball and turned towards the house.

'Alice!' he shouted.

Beethoven grabbed the ball and tried to give it back to Mr Newton, but the door slammed in his face. Beethoven sat down and waited. Eventually the door would open up again.

Inside, the hall was jammed with Newtons, young and old. Ted was rummaging through the cupboard looking for his baseball glove – team try-outs were that day.

Emily and Ryce were busy packing their school bags. Mrs Newton, who helped out at Newton Air Freshners, was getting together the charts and graphs that they would need when they made their presentation to Mr Bickert at the bank. George was rubbing frantically at the stains on his suit.

'Are you going to change your clothes?' Mrs Newton asked her husband. 'Should I get your blue blazer?'

Mr Newton shook his head vigorously. 'No. If this meeting is going to determine the future of our company, I'm going to wear my lucky suit.'

Suddenly, Emily dug deep into her school bag and pulled out something tiny and shiny and held it up to her father. 'Would you like to borrow my lucky penny, Daddy?'

'Yes.' George Newton took the penny and put it in his pocket. He figured he needed all the help he could get. 'Thank you, Emily.'

'Hey,' Ted called from the deepest recesses of the hall cupboard, 'has anyone seen my baseball glove?'

Just then, the doorbell rang and Ryce jumped to answer it. On the porch stood a tall, blond eighteen-year-old boy. He had blue eyes and a dazzling smile. Ryce's heart melted a little bit when she saw Taylor Devereaux and she moved her mouth to say something – but she was so flustered no sound came out.

'Hi,' said Taylor. 'Michelle said you could use a lift to school.'

Ryce managed to calm down long enough to pull together some lame words. 'Yeah . . . uh, hi . . . Um, Mom . . . Dad . . . this is –'

Taylor was a master at the art of charming parents. 'Hi. I'm Taylor Devereaux,' he said, shaking Mr Newton's hand firmly. 'And you have my word that Ryce will get to school and back again in perfect safety.'

'That's good,' said Mrs Newton evenly, 'because if she didn't I would be forced to firebomb your bedroom.'

Ryce blushed, embarrassed that her mother had said such a thing – but, then again, she would have been embarrassed no matter what her mother said. But Taylor just laughed.

'Boy,' he said to Ryce. 'You didn't tell me

about your mom. She's not just prettier than my mom, she's funnier too.'

Mrs Newton laughed. 'OK, you can live. In fact, if you want, you can live here.' She patted Ryce on the back. 'OK, go on. Have a nice day at school.'

Ryce grinned and ran out of the house with Taylor. Both Mr Newton and Beethoven watched them go, neither man nor dog quite sure if he trusted the charming teenage boy.

'I don't like it,' said Mr Newton.

'Come on,' said his wife. 'He's giving her a lift to school. You used to give me lifts to school.'

'Yes,' said George, nodding. 'But that was different.'

'How?' his wife challenged.

'This kid has a convertible. A power-blue convertible. That makes all the difference.'

'So it's blue,' said Mrs Newton. 'You had a blue bike.'

'The convertible isn't just *blue*,' replied Mr Newton. 'It's *powder* blue. There's big difference between ordinary, run of the mill blue and *powder* blue.'

Suddenly, Emily tugged at her mother's sleeve. 'Mom, are we late for school yet?'

Alice Newton didn't even have to look at her watch. 'Oh my gosh . . .'

Suddenly, all the Newtons, Beethoven included, were rushing out of the front door. Everyone had something to carry, and Beethoven had his ball. He nudged it into Emily's hand and gave her a pleading look, begging her to play with him before it was too late.

Emily took pity on her big furry friend – school could wait one more second.

'OK, Beethoven,' she said. She threw the ball as hard as she could, and it sailed over the fence into the garden of the house next door. Beethoven took off after it like a bullet, delighted that someone had *finally* thrown the ball for him.

Mrs Newton was about to get into the car. 'Emily, we're late! C'mon!'

'Coming!' Emily scrambled into the car, and they pulled out of the driveway.

They were out of sight by the time Beethoven squeezed through the fence, the ball in his mouth. He was panting and his eyes were bright with happiness as he looked around for Emily, to show the little girl that he had fetched the ball for her.

But she was nowhere to be seen. Beethoven trotted up the porch and scratched at the door – maybe she had gone inside. But the house was silent.

Beethoven blinked and sighed in disappointment, the ball tumbling from his mouth. He sat down on the porch and put his head on his paws. It would be a long time before his family returned and he got lonely without them.

Then, suddenly, Beethoven had an idea. He would take a walk around the neighbourhood to see if he could find someone else to play with. After all, not *everyone* had to go to school.

Chapter 4

It wasn't in Beethoven's nature to be unhappy for very long, but he had to admit that he did feel a little low that morning. He was lonely. All the Newtons had someplace to be and something to do – they were far too busy to play with him. As Beethoven patrolled his neighbourhood, he started to notice that everyone had someone – except him.

The first thing he saw was a cute couple, a man and a woman, walking hand in hand down the street. They were trailed by their dogs, two cute, curly-haired poodles. They looked like a very happy family. Beethoven sighed forlornly. No room for him there . . .

In the park, he saw an elderly couple sitting on a bench. They looked like they had been married for a very long time, and Beethoven could tell by their exchange of tender looks and affectionate smiles that they were still very much in love. Beethoven sighed heavily. He wished he were in love.

But at least he had a friend! Racing across the grass came the little white dog called Sparky. Sparky was an old friend of Beethoven's – they had been puppies together – and they had shared many adventures. Beethoven was very happy to see his pal. He barked cheerfully to get Sparky's attention.

But Sparky didn't even see Beethoven! Sprinting along next to him was a cute little female dog – Sparky was on a date! He only had eyes for his companion, and they raced right past Beethoven without even stopping to sniff.

Beethoven sighed heavily and looked up into the trees. But what he saw there made him feel even worse. Nestled on the branch of a big oak tree were two turtle doves, billing and cooing. Even the birds had companions, but Beethoven had no one. He felt very sorry for himself.

But things were about to change . . .

Beethoven was walking slowly out of the park when suddenly he stopped and sniffed the breeze. There was a wonderful smell – wonderful to a St Bernard, anyway. Then he heard a man's voice calling to someone.

'Heeere, Missy! C'mon, girl!'

Beethoven's ears twitched and perked up. Turning around, he saw a beautiful female St Bernard running across the field towards her owner. Beethoven gazed at this beautiful girl and felt light-headed, dazed at this glorious vision in red-and-white fur. Music seemed to swell up and fill his ears, and the earth seemed to move under his feet.

It only took one look and Beethoven knew! At last! He had found his life's companion! The girl of his dreams! His tail wagged happily and his eyes shone brightly.

Beethoven watched, lovesick already, as the lovely animal ran up to her owner. He was a short, kind-looking man named Mr Brillo – Beethoven had seen him in the neighbourhood, but he didn't know he had a pet, never mind a St Bernard. It was obvious that he loved his big dog. Mr Brillo knelt down and patted her affectionately.

'Hey, Missy,' he said, 'let's go over to the ice-cream van and get ourselves a treat.'

Beethoven started bounding towards the pair, a funny little purring sound – if you could say dogs purred – issuing from deep within his throat.

'So, Missy,' Mr Brillo was saying just as Beethoven arrived. 'What kind of ice-cream do you want? Vanilla or chocolate?'

Missy thought for a moment.

'It takes a little time for her to make up her mind,' Mr Brillo told the man in the ice-cream van.

'Take your time,' he said.

Then Missy barked once.

The man grinned, as if he understood dog language. 'You got it! One strawberry cone!'

But Missy suddenly wasn't very interested in an ice-cold treat. She was looking at Beethoven, who was coming towards her, and she could feel her heart thumping in her chest. She wasn't paying any attention to Mr Brillo.

Her master was looking at Beethoven too. 'Hey there, big fella,' he said. 'How are you doing today? Just out for a little walk? Missy, you know this guy?'

But Missy didn't answer. She just sat on her haunches, her tail wagging happily. The two dogs were unable to take their eyes off each other.

'Missy,' said Mr Brillo. 'Hello? Remember me?'

But Missy was deaf to her owner. She tilted her head, and then an affectionate little growl rose in her throat and she rubbed her nose against Beethoven's soft ear.

For a moment, Beethoven thought he would faint with happiness. He leaned forward and gave a hesitant little lick on Missy's cheek. Missy nuzzled into him and gave him a lick back. A look of pure joy crossed Beethoven's face. His eyes were bright and he gave out an ecstatic little yelp. There was no doubt in his mind or in his heart – he was in love! And things had looked so bleak just a few minutes before.

Mr Brillo shook his head and shrugged. 'Better make that two strawberry cones,' he told the man in the ice-cream van.

'Right!'

Mr Brillo took the cones and knelt down next to the two love-struck dogs. He held one of the treats out to each of them.

'OK. This one is on me . . .'

At the same time, Missy and Beethoven leaned forward, and with one quick whisk of their big pink tongues, they whipped the ice-cream right out of the cones. Without taking their eyes off each other, they gulped down the treat.

Mr Brillo laughed and ruffled the fur on the back of Beethoven's neck.

Suddenly, a red car, a Lexus, screamed around the corner and screeched to a halt right next to the ice-cream van. A man was driving, and there was a woman in the passenger seat. She jumped out of the car the instant the car stopped.

Mr Brillo's kindly face fell when he saw the woman. 'Regina,' he said weakly. 'What a . . . pleasant . . . surprise. Or something.'

Beethoven looked at the woman and decided he didn't like what he saw. She was very thin, with bony, sharp features that gave her a mean, spiteful look. Her hair was dyed red and her fingernails were the color of blood. Clutched in one hand was a thick chrome chain. In the other was a heavy alligator-skin handbag.

'This is no surprise, Brillo,' she said. Her voice was angry and harsh. 'You knew I was supposed to meet you here. Time's up. Your visit with this mutt is over.'

Mr Brillo sadly looked at his watch. How quickly the time had passed . . .

'Regina,' said Mr Brillo, 'what do you want Missy for? You hate dogs. You hate all living things.'

Regina bent down and roughly snapped the chain around Missy's neck. Beethoven felt a sudden stab of anger and he growled menacingly.

Regina ignored him. 'Listen, Brillo, I got the court order, so the dog stays in the apartment with me while we negotiate our little divorce settlement!'

'Regina . . .' said Mr Brillo pleadingly.

'Don't Regina me. You clear on what I want?'

Mr Brillo nodded. 'Yeah. Everything.' Mr Brillo didn't really look it, but he was pretty rich. And he was prepared to give up a large part of his fortune to get his beloved dog out of the clutches of his soon-to-be-ex-wife.

'That's right,' Regina snarled. 'Everything I can get.' She yanked hard on the chain, trying to drag Missy towards her car. But Missy didn't want to go.

Regina didn't have a lot of patience. Without warning, she whacked Missy on the side of the head with her heavy handbag. Missy winced and whimpered. 'Move it, stupid!'

'Regina!' yelled Mr Brillo.

In a flash, Beethoven jumped forward, pulled the handbag from Regina's hand and dumped it on the ground. The woman turned and yelled.

'Floyd! Get over here!'

A muscle-bound guy with a lot of gold chains around his neck got out of the car. He looked strong but stupid. Floyd towered over Mr Brillo.

'How's it goin', shorty?'

'Get the dog in the car,' ordered Regina.

'No *problemo*,' said Floyd. He took hold of Missy's chain and dragged her towards the car. He opened the rear door and shoved the dog inside.

Very carefully, Regina leaned down to get her handbag. Beethoven had his eyes locked on the woman, and he was growling. 'You stay away from me,' she said.

Beethoven growled even louder.

'Brillo,' said Regina, 'you want your dog back

– then talk to my lawyer.' Without another word, Regina got in the car and drove away.

Mr Brillo rested his hand on Beethoven's head. 'Rule number one – never get married when you're drunk.'

But Beethoven wasn't listening. He was watching the red Lexus race away. Suddenly, Beethoven was off and running, chasing the car. He had a very determined look on his face – he had waited too long to find his love to lose her now.

Chapter 5

Out on the edge of town at the air freshener factory, Mr Newton and his wife were doing their best to convince Mr Bickert, the banker, that they had a great new idea to expand their business.

Mr Newton had done a lot of thinking about air fresheners and he realized that wherever air met bad smells there was room for one of his new products.

Mr Bickert sat in George Newton's office listening to the sales pitch, but he didn't look convinced. Spread out in front of him on the table was a mass of papers, the financial statements of the Newton Air Freshener Company. Standing in a corner of the room were two easels with black cloths draped over them, hiding the charts propped up on them. Beyond the office, he could see the machinery of the factory stamping out little green air fresheners.

Mr Newton was talking excitedly. 'I want to put air fresheners where air fresheners have never been put before.'

'Is that so?' said Mr Bickert politely. But it didn't seem to Mrs Newton, who was watching her husband's performance, that the banker was terribly interested in George Newton's vision.

'Yes!' Mr Newton pounded his fist on the table, making Mr Bickert jump. 'I want to put a Newton air freshener in every health club, in every locker room in America.'

'Health clubs?' asked Mr Bickert.

'That's right.' George nodded towards Mrs Newton, giving her the signal to pull the black cloths off the easels. Underneath were two big cardboard illustrations showing dozens of air fresheners – but air fresheners were usually shaped like little pine trees. These, on the other hand, were shaped like sporting goods: baseballs, basketballs, barbells and tennis rackets. There were even some shaped like famous athletes.

George Newton beamed at the little pictures. 'Newton sports fresheners!' he said triumphantly.

If Mr Bickert was impressed, he didn't show it.

But Mr Newton had more tricks up his sleeve. He snatched a sports bag off his desk and held it under Mr Bickert's nose.

'Here,' said George Newton, 'have a sniff of this!'

Very reluctantly, Mr Bickert lowered his head and took a prissy little sniff of the bag. Then he recoiled in horror as if the bag were filled with rotting fish.

'Stinks, doesn't it?'

'Indeed!' agreed Mr Bickert.

'That bag contains an unwashed jockstrap, old underwear and a three-day-old cheese sandwich. It all belongs to my son,' said Mrs Newton.

Mr Bickert looked alarmed.

'But what's the solution to this smell, you may ask?' said Mr Newton. 'It's easy' – he grabbed one of the new air fresheners, this one shaped like a football, and tossed it into the bag – 'all you have to do is throw in a Newton.'

'That's all?' asked Mr Bickert.

George Newton's voice was full of pride. 'That's it.' He thrust the bag under the banker's nose. '*Now* take a whiff.'

Mr Bickert really didn't want to smell Ted's sports bag again, but he didn't see how he could avoid it. Very hesitantly he took a sniff and immediately looked impressed. The nasty smell was gone, replaced by the nice aroma of fresh leather. It was as if there were a brand-new football in the bag.

'Now,' said Mr Newton, 'is that pigskin or is that pigskin?'

'Amazing!' said Mr Bickert.

'You see!' said George Newton, gratified by the banker's response. 'We're planning a signature line – air fresheners with the faces of real athletes, like the NBA's Charles Barkley and Joe Montana.'

'Really?' asked the banker. 'And what will they smell like?'

George Newton leaned forward. 'They'll smell like Charles Barkley and Joe Montana.'

Mr Bickert looked bewildered for a moment, staring into Mr Newton's eyes. George was keeping an absolutely straight face and the banker couldn't tell if he was joking or not. The whole idea was so crazy that it might be a joke . . . but then again, it might not.

'Are . . . are you serious?'

Suddenly, Mr Newton began to laugh. 'No, of course not – but I am serious about making these sports fresheners. And if we can get celebrity endorsements, so much the better. We know it's a winner, Mr Bickert.'

'Well, the smell test is certainly impressive.'

'And all we need is two hundred thousand dollars. That will cover retooling and new machinery.'

'And another two hundred thousand,' put in Mrs Newton, 'for promotion. We want to go on television to advertise this. We're sure these things can take off.'

Suddenly Mr Bickert looked very serious. 'That kind of money is a problem for me. Your company's credit is already overextended, and with the cash flow you've had in the last few months . . .' The banker shook his head. 'I'm sorry, but no matter how great your idea might be, the company is too much of a risk.'

Alice Newton looked worried. Mr Bickert sounded as if he had made up his mind and nothing would change it. But that didn't stop her husband from trying.

'But the time is so *right* for this,' he said pleadingly. 'I know it is. I'd stake my life on it.'

'Really?' said Mr Bickert.

'Absolutely!'

The banker leaned forward in his seat. 'Look, I can see that you're committed to putting these things in the market-place and, in a strange way, you might even have a pretty good chance of making some money with them. But you just don't qualify for a loan from my bank. At least, your *company* doesn't qualify . . .'

'What do you mean?' asked Alice Newton.

'Well, you said you'd stake your life on this product . . . Your *personal* credit is fine. I could make this loan to you as individuals.'

'I still don't understand.'

'It would be simple. You put up your house as collateral and you get your money. But if the product flops, you run the risk of losing your home.'

Mr and Mrs Newton exchanged nervous glances. Suddenly this wasn't fun any more.

'I think we might have to talk this over, Mr Bickert,' said Alice Newton slowly. 'We'll have to get back to you . . .'

Running as fast as he could, Beethoven kept the red Lexus in sight, following it across town to a fancy neighbourhood of tall apartment buildings.

The car stopped in front of one of them. Beethoven watched as Regina got out of the car, followed by the big man, Floyd, who yanked Missy by her chain, making her follow him into the building.

Silently, Beethoven followed them but by the time he got close to the apartment block, the big glass doors had swung shut, locking him out of the lobby of the building. Beethoven sighed as he peered through the glass, watching the bad guys and his beloved disappear into the elevator.

But he wasn't beaten yet! Quickly he raced around the corner to the rear of the apartment block . . .

Floyd followed Regina into her apartment, pulling Missy behind him.

'Are you sure this plan will work?' he asked. 'It's only a dog. So he misses her. Big deal. Brillo will get over it.'

Regina was admiring herself in the mirror in the hall of the apartment. She never got tired of looking at herself. 'Sweetie,' she said without taking her eyes off herself, 'he doesn't miss that dog. He *lives* for that dog.' Regina patted her hair into place.

'And after I let him see her a few more times, we hide her away somewhere, after which he falls apart like a little boy and pays exactly one million dollars to divorce me. Then, and only then, he gets the dog back.'

Floyd pulled Missy across the room and then knelt to unclip the chain on her collar. 'If the guy was smart, he'd take the million beans and buy himself some real farm animals.'

'Get that dumb animal out of here. She's gonna shed all over everything,' said Regina, looking at Missy with distaste.

'Right, doll,' said Floyd. He pushed open the sliding door that opened on to the balcony, and then he shoved Missy outside, closing the door firmly behind her.

Missy looked sad as she sat down on the cold concrete of the balcony floor. Then she heard a sound that made her heart leap with joy. It was Beethoven barking!

She jumped to her feet and peered over the railing of the balcony. Three storeys down she saw Beethoven, sitting on the apartment block lawn staring up at her. The moment he caught sight of his beloved, Beethoven's tail began to wag and he barked happily. Missy barked back, her eyes bright. It was a sort of doggy *Romeo and Juliet*!

Now it was Beethoven to the rescue! He raced up the concrete fire stairs, quickly climbing up to the landing on Missy's floor. The trouble was, there was a big gap between the stairs and Missy's balcony – and a big drop to the ground below.

Beethoven didn't hesitate. He made a great big running jump and vaulted the space separating him from his new girlfriend. He landed at Missy's feet. The two dogs were delighted to see each other, and they happily licked each other's faces.

Beethoven knew they had to get out of there quickly. He sprang up on to the wall lining the balcony and barked encouragement to Missy. She looked at him nervously, but he begged her with his brown eyes to follow him. He had to get her away from those terrible people!

It took all her courage, but finally Missy jumped up on to the wall next to Beethoven, and together they sprang across the open space to freedom.

Quickly, they scurried down the fire escape steps and ran away. Beethoven barked with delight – he was reunited with his love!

Chapter 6

It was not a good day for Ted Newton. His greatest fantasy was to make the school baseball team. He knew his chances weren't that great, but he was determined to try. It took all of Ted's courage to go to the try-outs which were being held after school, but he forced himself to go.

When he got to the baseball field he found things pretty much as he had expected them to be. There were a dozen boys with baseball gloves spread out across the diamond and a coach who was hitting flies to the outfield. Ted was the smallest kid there, but that wasn't the worst of it.

Gathered in the stands were a group of girls from his class who had stayed around after school to watch the try-outs. Ted wasn't very sure of himself around girls, although he was sure he wanted to get to know girls better. Girls, on the other hand, usually ignored him completely, favouring the bigger, cooler boys in the class. Sometimes they even made fun of him.

When the coach put Ted into centre-field there was giggling from the stands.

'Hey, look! Newton's trying out for the team!'

exclaimed one of the girls. This set off gales of snickering.

'Newton! You're dreaming!'

Ted just ignored them – but he was glad that he was far out in the outfield so they couldn't see that he had blushed all the way up to his ears!

The coach was hitting the fly balls high and far, and a couple of times Ted circled under them, his glove raised ready to catch the ball. Except the other kids in the outfield kept on bumping him out of the way and snagging the flies that Ted was *sure* he could have caught.

Ted could hear the kids in the stands laughing among themselves. Ted just thumped his glove and tried to shut out the sound of their giggles.

The coach, at home plate, could see what was going on and decided to give Ted a chance.

'Newton! This one is for you!' He smacked a ball hard and it sailed high into the blue sky. Everyone on the field stopped and watched, following the ball into the air, then watching as Ted shaded his eyes against the sun.

'It's gonna drop in front of you, Newton!' shouted one of the boys.

'Move in! Move in!'

'Yeah! Move in, Newton!'

Ted hesitated for a moment, afraid that the kids were deliberately misleading him – they hadn't been nice to him at all that afternoon, so why should things change now? Then he realized that they were right, the ball was going to fall. If this had been a real game it would have dropped in for a hit.

Suddenly, Ted was off and running, sprinting full out, his glove held stretched out in front of him. The ball was coming down fast, so all Ted could do was make a leaping grab and hope for the best.

Ted slid on his chest and his glasses flew off – but not before he caught a glimpse of the ball bouncing a few feet ahead of him. All of the kids on the field burst out laughing. Even the coach had to smirk a little. Ted looked awkward and ridiculous and he knew it.

The coach was already packing up the equipment. 'Maybe next year, Newton. OK, everybody, try-outs are over!'

Humiliated, Ted grabbed his glasses and walked off the field. He didn't look left or right and did his best to avoid making eye contact with any of the kids who were still standing around. It seemed like every kid in the entire world was friends with some other kid – except him.

Ted plodded home slowly. With each step he felt more miserable. Ted was small and unsure of himself, and he couldn't play any sport to save his life. Worse than that, he was good in class – algebra, history, science, he could handle them all – and that seemed to make him even more unpopular. He couldn't help it if he was clever. It just wasn't his fault . . .

By the time Ted got home, he knew there was only one thing that would make him feel better. A big hug from his best friend – Beethoven.

But after Ted searched high and low, he realized that Beethoven was nowhere to be found. Ted sat down on the front porch steps of his house and let out a big, soul-wrenching, Beethoven-sized sigh.

Beethoven had no idea his young friend was so dejected and depressed. If he had known, he would have been very upset. But right at that moment, Beethoven had never been happier!

Missy and Beethoven had made their escape – Regina and Floyd didn't even know she was gone – and were busy romping through the streets of the town, wandering and watching the humans. And falling deeper and deeper in puppy love.

As the youngest child, Emily was put to bed first. She had fallen asleep half in and half out of her bed, and her parents went upstairs to cover her up properly and make sure that the little girl slept comfortably.

Since their meeting that morning with the banker, Alice and George had talked nonstop about what Mr Bickert had said about borrowing money by putting their house up as collateral. They even talked about it while putting Emily to bed.

'I know it's a risk,' Alice Newton whispered as she fluffed Emily's pillows. 'But I think we have to take the risk.'

'You do?' her husband whispered back. He straightened his daughter's sheets and together, Alice and George tiptoed towards the door.

'Sure,' she said. 'If things keep going the way they have been, we would end up selling the house anyway . . .'

'Probably,' George Newton admitted, closing the door to Emily's room behind him. They were out in the hall now, and they could speak in their normal voices.

Mrs Newton shrugged. 'My feeling is, we take our best shot and see what happens.'

George stopped in the hallway and took his wife in his arms. His words came from the heart. 'You know, even if things didn't work out, doing without some of the things we have now wouldn't be the end of the world. As long as you and I and the kids are together . . .'

Alice kissed him gently on the lips. 'Don't worry, honey. Things will work out. I'm sure they will.'

Ted emerged from his bedroom and joined his mother and father at the top of the stairs.

'What will?' he asked.

'Business things,' said George.

But before Ted could ask any more questions, the quiet of the night was broken by the sound of a powerful car pulling up in front of the Newton house. Curious, Ted and his parents peered out of the window just in time to see Taylor Devereaux's powder-blue Camaro pull up to the kerb.

'Now what?' asked George.

Ryce was embarrassed and enthralled at the same time. She had gone out right after dinner, telling her parents that she was going over to Michelle's house to study – that was true. What she hadn't told George and Alice was that Taylor Devereaux was going to give her a lift home when the study session was over.

She was excited that the coolest guy in her class was paying so much attention to her, but she was embarrassed that he had driven her home so . . . noisily. She glanced nervously at the house when the car stopped. Her mom and dad must have heard the loud engine.

But Ryce couldn't worry about that now. Right then, the most important thing on her mind was saying good-night to Taylor without saying something stupid or acting like a complete dork.

She looked down at the pile of schoolbooks in her lap. 'Well,' she said softly, 'thanks for the lift.'

But Taylor seemed to be in the mood to talk. 'You know, I saw you up in the mountains last summer. Do your folks have a cottage up there or something?'

Ryce shook her head. 'No. We just rented one for a week. Summer vacation.'

Taylor nodded and inched a little closer to Ryce on the car seat. 'The reason I remember is because . . . when I saw you last summer, I had this thought . . .'

Ryce shot him a sideways glance. She was curious but at the same time she didn't want to seem too eager. 'Really?'

'Yeah, really. Wouldn't you like to know what I was thinking?'

Ryce shrugged as if she didn't really care one way or another – although inside she was dying of curiosity. 'Sure. I mean, it's up to you.'

46

Taylor moved a little closer and his arm snaked across the top of the seat. 'I thought, I wonder if she's ever been kissed. *That's* what I thought.'

Ryce was totally unprepared for this development. Her eyes grew wide. 'Really?'

'Have you?'

For a moment, Ryce almost panicked. In fact, she had never been kissed by a boy – but she was afraid to say so. What if he laughed at her? On the other hand, she couldn't lie about it – what if he called her bluff? All of this raced through her mind, but Ryce decided that honesty was the best policy.

She shook her head slowly. 'No,' she said.

The next few seconds seemed to pass as if they were in a dream. Very slowly, Taylor leaned over Ryce and kissed her warmly and softly on her lips. Ryce closed her eyes.

Later, she would not be able to tell how long the kiss had lasted – it felt as if it went on for ever, but also as if it passed in a split second.

When Taylor pulled back from her, he noticed that her eyes were still closed. He smiled to himself.

'I'll see you tomorrow,' he said.

'OK,' said Ryce, her eyes still closed.

She opened them to get out of the car, though, and, in a complete daze, she tried to stroll casually up the driveway, as if nothing out of the ordinary had happened. However, as her feet hit the ground, her knees almost gave out, as if her legs were asleep, and she felt so light-headed from the kiss that she thought she might faint. So, instead of a breezy amble up to the house, Ryce managed something between tiptoes and a stagger.

She found her parents waiting for her, eyeing their daughter curiously. But Ryce didn't even notice. She walked straight by them, like a sleep-walker.

'Hi, Mom, hi, Dad,' she said dreamily.

'I thought you said you were studying with Michelle,' said Alice Newton.

Ryce put her books down on the table in the hall and smiled happily at her parents. 'I was.'

'So who dropped you off?' asked George.

'Taylor,' said Ryce, heading for the stairs. Even though she was still in a trance, she knew instinctively that the less she told her parents the better.

'Well,' said Alice, standing at the bottom of the stairs. 'Was he studying too?'

Ryce stopped and blinked. 'I don't know.'

What an odd question, she thought. Why would someone as perfect as Taylor Devereaux need to do something as ordinary as study?

*

Ryce was not the only Newton with love on the brain that night. Beethoven and Missy had wandered to the outskirts of town, to the Starlight Drive-In Cinema. The two big dogs had squeezed through a hole in the fence and found themselves a cosy little spot where they could watch the movie. But Beethoven realized there was something missing . . .

He wandered away for a moment, searching a nearby rubbish bin until he came up with an almost full tub of popcorn. What was a movie without popcorn?

Beethoven put the popcorn down in front of his beloved, and Missy gratefully took a mouthful. Then she leaned her big head against Beethoven's neck and relaxed, watching the movie screen and sighing contentedly. Beethoven's heart beat faster - he had never been so happy before in his life.

On the big drive-in screen, the two stars were coming to the big moment of the story – and it perfectly mirrored the moment between Beethoven and Missy.

'I love you,' the male actor said.

'I love *you*,' said the female lead.

Then the music swelled up dramatically, and the two humans kissed. Suddenly, to Beethoven, the whole night seemed filled with music and love and stars.

Missy turned and touched her nose to Beethoven's and he jumped slightly, as if he had been shocked. No instant in time, he thought, could ever be as perfect as this one – but, as he was to learn, the whole night turned out to be perfect . . .

Ten Weeks Later . . .

Chapter 7

George Newton had never been so busy, or so excited, in his life. In the last two-and-a-half months so much had changed. He and Alice had decided to go ahead with the decision to borrow money against their house, and as soon as the first cheques had arrived Mr Newton had worked around the clock.

The old machinery in the factory had been taken out and new pieces were arriving every day. Even the name of the company had changed. Gone was boring old Newton Air Fresheners and in its place a sleek new logo and the name Newton Sports Fresheners. A lot of people probably wouldn't have noticed the change, but to George Newton the switch was earth-shaking.

When it came to changing the face of the air freshener business, George was a ball of energy. He didn't even mind getting dirty!

The day the new machinery arrived, he climbed up on to the trucks and started unloading the heavy equipment himself. His employees helped as best they could, but not one of them could keep up with the boss.

George, his tie loosened and his suit jacket off, carried a piece of machinery down from the bed of a truck. Billy, the factory foreman, tried to give him a hand, but Mr Newton waved him off.

Just then a secretary emerged from the offices clutching a cellular phone. 'Mr Newton! It's your call from New York.'

George Newton jumped down from the truck and grabbed the phone. 'Yes?' He listened for a moment, his face darkening. 'A million dollars? Charles Barkley wants a million dollars to appear on my sports freshener? Get lost! I've got hockey players who'd give their dentures to get their face put on a Newton sports freshener.'

Mr Newton's shoulders slumped. How could it be that some people just didn't understand his vision? He allowed himself a moment or two to feel sorry for himself and then returned to his machinery. There was still a lot of work to be done . . .

By five o'clock that evening, the new machinery had been installed. There was still much more to be done, of course, but not even George could force himself to do any more work without having some rest.

Exhausted, he managed to stagger home, hoping to snatch a little sleep before starting work all over again.

When he got back to the house he found Alice sitting at the dining-room table, her cheque-book, bills and pocket calculator spread out in front of her.

'George,' she said, alarmed at the tired look in his eyes. 'Are you all right?'

'It's done,' he said wearily. 'We're all set up. Everything is finally in place.'

'Oh, honey! That's wonderful.'

Unable to take another step, George Newton slumped down in one of the dining chairs. 'Gosh, am I tired . . .'

'Can I get you anything?' Mrs Newton asked.

George nodded. 'More than anything else in the world, right now I'd like a hug. A family hug.'

Alice jumped to her feet and shouted, 'Everybody! Quick! Daddy needs a hug!'

There was silence from the rest of the house.

'Uh . . . kids?'

Ryce called from the kitchen, 'I'm on the phone.'

Emily was in the family room watching TV. 'I'll give him one at the next commercial.'

Ted shouted from upstairs. 'I'll be down in a few minutes.'

George Newton looked sadly at his wife. 'But I need a hug,' he said plaintively.

Suddenly, Beethoven appeared in the dining-room doorway. Hug was definitely a concept he understood – in fact, if anyone was an expert at giving hugs, it was Beethoven. Like they say: the bigger the dog, the bigger the love . . .

Beethoven charged straight at George, barrelling right at him, throwing himself at his weary master. All of a sudden George was enveloped in a furry embrace as Beethoven wrapped his paws around George's shoulders, pinning him to the wall. Beethoven's big, pink, warm tongue slapped across his face like a paintbrush.

'Aaaarrggghhh!' spluttered Mr Newton as man and dog landed in a tangled heap on the floor. 'Get off me!'

He managed to wrestle his pet off him, then he dragged himself to his feet. 'Well,' said George. 'I feel so much better.'

The next morning, Ted was playing furiously with his hand-held computer game when Emily came in and sat down next to him on the couch. 'Have you seen Beethoven?'

Ted didn't even look up from his game. 'Not since yesterday. He must be around some-where.'

Emily shook her head vigorously. 'No, he's not. I looked everywhere.'

Ted kept on playing. 'He'll show up, Emily.'

'And d'you know what else? He's been sneaking out of the house at night too.'

'How do you know?' said Ted without looking up.

'A noise woke me up last night and I saw him out my window. He was sneaking out of the garden.'

Ted stopped playing and thought a moment. 'Well, maybe he's visiting some other family. Some people who feed him more than we do.'

Emily shook her head again. 'That's not it.' Then she went very still. 'Sssh - I hear something.'

As Ted looked up, the sound of paw steps could be heard coming up the basement steps into the kitchen. Tiptoeing from the living-room, down the hall, Ted and Emily stopped and peeked in.

Beethoven was lapping some water from his bowl, but he was doing it in a secret, most un-Beethovenish kind of way. He looked over his shoulder, as if checking to see if anyone was watching him. But he didn't notice the two kids.

Then he took the big bone from his bowl and carried it back down the basement stairs.

Ted and Emily exchanged looks.

'Come on,' Ted said. 'Let's follow him.' They crept down the stairs just in time to see Beethoven hop up on to the work-bench and squirm out of the basement window.

Ted pulled Emily back up the steps, and they ran around the house and saw Beethoven confidently trotting across the driveway and then sauntering down the pavement.

'Let's get my bike,' whispered Ted.

Beethoven seemed very intent on getting where he was going and getting there as soon as possible. He didn't look back as he loped down the main street of town. He didn't even notice Ted and Emily ten or twelve yards behind him. Ted was standing up and pedalling his bike and Emily was clinging to the seat as they chased after their dog.

Beethoven made his way to the same apartment building where Regina and Floyd had taken Missy a couple of days before. But he walked by the main entrance of the building and, instead, headed down the sloped ramp leading down into the apartment block's underground garage.

'Where's he going?' Emily asked. 'What's he up to?'

'I don't know.' Ted stopped pedalling and coasted to a halt next to the entrance to the garage. Emily hopped off the bike and he stashed it under a bush. Tiptoeing forward, they peeked down the driveway.

Beethoven was sitting in front of the sliding door of the garage, the bone still clutched in his mouth, waiting patiently for the door to open.

Suddenly, from inside the garage, Ted and Emily could hear a car engine start and, a moment later, the hum of machinery as the big door started to retract into the ceiling. The gap between the edge of the door and the concrete floor was no more than a foot when Beethoven ran to it and scrambled under, disappearing into the dark interior.

'C'mon!' said Ted, pulling his sister towards the garage. Together they ran down the sloping ramp. They had to stop and flatten themselves against the wall to let the car pass. The door had stopped moving, and Ted and Emily hoped that it would stay open long enough for them to get inside the garage.

But a moment later, with a grinding sound, the door started to descend again. Ted and Emily watched it, scared now, not sure if they should attempt to get into the garage or not. They were both dying of curiosity, anxious to know why Beethoven was behaving so strangely – but at the same time, they didn't want to get stuck in a garage. It would be dark in there . . .

'Should we be doing this?' asked Ted.

'Yes,' said Emily. She grabbed her brother by the hand and they ran hard for the garage door, reaching it just in time to scramble underneath.

The door closed with a thud. They were trapped.

Chapter 8

Regina and Floyd had been looking forward to this day for weeks. The cottage up at the lake was waiting for them, and all they had to do was head up there and lay low for a while until Mr Brillo became so desperate for Missy that he would pay any price to get her back. There was just one problem – Missy was missing.

'I'm going to kill that stupid dog!' fumed Regina. She was sitting at her kitchen table furiously working on a sign with a big, thick, black Magic Marker: LOST – FEMALE ST BERNARD. NAME – MISSY. CASH REWARD!

'I just hope Brillo doesn't discover that I've lost his precious dog. That would ruin everything,' she muttered.

Floyd wasn't really paying too much attention. He was busy flexing his muscles in front of the hall mirror. 'Tell me, do you think I'm getting too bulky?'

Regina threw down her pen in disgust. 'Listen, Mr New Jersey,' she snapped, 'until we get that dog back, I am short of one million dollars!'

Floyd flexed a little more. 'Regina,' he said

soothingly. 'Relax. Dogs come back. They're stupid. That makes them loyal.'

'Sounds a lot like someone I know,' Regina grumbled. She returned to her sign, but she was interrupted by a knock at her front door.

Regina flung open the door. Standing there was an elderly man in stained blue denim overalls. It was Gus, the janitor of her apartment building. He was a frail old gent, and he looked genuinely afraid of Regina – of course, most people *were* afraid of Regina.

'Yeah? What is it? What do you want?' she demanded.

It took a moment for him to find his voice, a split-second delay that made her even more angry. 'C'mon, spit it out!'

'I . . . I just wanted to tell you, I found your dog. She's downstairs in the basement furnace room.'

This was a piece of good news and Regina did her best not to be mad at the old man but, as she *was* generally angry at the world no matter what, this was far from easy for her. 'Good! Thank you.' She turned. 'Floyd. Put the suitcases in the car and bring it out front. We're finally getting out of here.'

Down in the basement, Beethoven had stopped

in front of a heavy iron door. It was shut tight. He was whimpering and scratching at it, pushing the barrier with his powerful body. But not even Beethoven could budge it.

Beethoven dropped his bone, took a step back and barked. From the other side, Missy barked back. Beethoven begged her to open the door, but Missy explained that she couldn't. She was trapped inside!

Ted and Emily peeked around the corner and saw their beloved dog urgently, frantically, scratching as if trying to burrow his way through. The boy and the girl knew they had to do something. They stepped out of their hiding-place.

'Hi, Beethoven,' said Emily.

For a moment, Beethoven seemed surprised to see them there – but he was also delighted. People may do strange things, he figured, but they also had strange powers – like the mysterious ability to open doors. Quickly, he licked Emily's hand and then barked at the door.

'We'd better open it for him,' said Emily, reaching for the door knob.

'Wait,' said Ted. There was a sign painted on the door and he pointed at it. 'See what it says?'

Reading wasn't Emily's strong suit yet, and she had to struggle to make sense of the big words. 'No un-author . . .'

'It says, "No Unauthorized Entry",' said Ted. 'That means we can't go in without permission.'

Emily looked around as if expecting to see someone who could give them permission. But there was no one else there except for Beethoven, who continued to scratch at the door intensely.

'No unauthorized entry,' said Emily. '*Unless* you have a really good reason.'

'Right,' said Ted, nodding in agreement.

Emily opened the door. Delighted, Beethoven grabbed his bone and squirmed through the space, Ted and Emily following close at his heels.

Missy and Beethoven were delighted to be reunited. After Beethoven dropped his bone at her feet, the two dogs licked each other, their tails wagging like palm trees in a hurricane.

'Look!' said Emily. 'Beethoven's got a friend!'

Ted, who was more worldly in these matters, said, 'He's got a *girlfriend*.'

Missy had picked up the bone and was running down the narrow corridor between the industrial-sized furnace and the wall. With a bark of encouragement to Ted and Emily, Beethoven trotted after her.

The passageway got narrower, and Ted and Emily had to crawl the last few feet between the heating ducts until they found themselves in a tiny space lit by a single dim light-bulb that hung from the dusty ceiling.

It took a moment for Ted and Emily's eyes to get used to the faint light, but when they did, they had the surprise of their lives. There, in the farthest corner of the little space were four tiny St Bernard puppies. The little dogs were trying to crawl and open their tiny eyes, but they were too weak to make even the tiniest little squeak.

Emily's eyes grew wide. 'Little Beethovens!' she said, amazed and delighted.

One puppy was the spitting image of Missy, with the same dark red colouring, but with big patches of white and brown. The next two looked like their dad. The fourth – the runt of the litter – was darker than his brothers and sisters, with almost no white fur at all.

The kids looked at Missy as she licked her puppies, and they patted Beethoven, who was sitting on his haunches looking every inch the proud father.

Ted hugged his dog. 'So, you and your girl-friend made some babies, huh, Beethoven?'

Beethoven gave a happy little bark, and Ted and Emily laughed out loud.

Then the kids felt their blood run cold. The door of the furnace room opened with a dull boom.

'Somebody in here?' Gus the janitor called out.

The kids jumped and grabbed the two big dogs, pulling them into the shadows to hide. Emily crouched down with her arms around Missy, while Ted knelt next to Beethoven.

Missy was very worried about her puppies, and she whimpered softly.

'Sssh,' Emily whispered in the dog's soft ear. 'We have to be very quiet.'

On the other side of the furnace, Regina took off her sunglasses and looked around. 'OK, Gus,' she snapped. 'Where's the dog?' She was carrying Missy's chain, and she rattled it in her hand.

Gus seemed a little confused. 'I don't know, ma'am. I left her right here. Maybe she went in behind the furnace.'

'Well, don't just stand there. Go and get her. I haven't got all day, you know.'

'Yes, ma'am.' Gus crouched down and squeezed behind the furnace. 'Here, doggie, doggie, doggie . . .'

'Tell me, Gus,' asked Regina disgustedly, 'how does someone like you manage to hold on to a job for more than a minute or two?'

The instant Beethoven heard Regina's voice, a low threatening growl rumbled out of his throat. Ted quickly put his hand over Beethoven's mouth. 'It's OK, boy,' he whispered in his ear. 'It's OK.'

Gus pulled a flashlight from his pocket and shone it into the narrow passage. He missed Ted and Emily and the dogs, but the beam settled on the puppies. At this early stage of their lives, the little puppies didn't know the difference between friend and foe, and so they clustered around Gus's boots as if he were an old pal of theirs.

'Uh – oh. You better come see this, ma'am . . .'

Regina took great care to make sure that she didn't touch any of the dusty walls. She took one look at the puppies and rolled her eyes.

'Where did these things come from?'

A puppy crawled on to one of her high-heeled shoes, and she shook it off with repugnance. 'Get away from me,' she shrieked angrily. 'Where's *my* dog, Gus? You know? The *big* one?'

Missy couldn't stand it any longer. Seeing the woman almost kick one of her little offspring, she broke from her hiding-place and rushed to her puppies. It took the combined strength of Ted and Emily to hold Beethoven back.

Forcing herself between Regina and her puppies, Missy barked one warning bark and then turned to her children, making sure they were all right.

'Well, Missy,' said Regina, 'aren't you just one great big pain in the butt.'

She leaned down and snapped the chain around her neck and yanked her out the musty corner of the furnace room. Gus laid a board across the opening to keep the puppies from following their mother. Missy managed to swivel her head to catch a glimpse of her little babies. She whined and whimpered as Regina pulled her away.

'What do you want me to do with those puppies?' asked Gus, trailing along behind Regina.

'I don't care,' said Regina over her shoulder. 'Just get rid of them. Take them to a shelter or something.'

'Animal shelters charge money to take in pups, ma'am,' said Gus.

'Money? No way! Not one penny from me. Just get rid of 'em. Drown 'em, why don't you?'

Emily and Ted exchanged horrified looks. It was all they could to hang on to Beethoven.

'The fewer dogs in this world the better, I say,' sneered Regina. 'Hey, wake up and give me a hand here, Gus.'

The old janitor caught up with Regina, grabbed on to the chain and helped the woman drag Missy out of the doorway. She was not going to go without a struggle, and she fought every step of the way through the door.

Together, Regina and Gus managed to muscle Missy out of the furnace room and into the garage. Behind them, the heavy iron door swung solidly shut.

'They're going to drown Beethoven's puppies!' gasped Emily, horror-struck at the very thought. 'We've got to get them out of here!'

'Right!' said Ted. He searched the gloomy little room until he found a dusty cardboard box. It was filled with rusty iron odds and ends – Ted figured they were probably old furnace parts – and he dumped them on the floor.

'Put the puppies in here,' he ordered Emily. Quickly, he stripped off his jacket and covered the box.

Beethoven wasn't paying any attention to all this activity. Rather, he was staring at the door, listening for any sign of Missy, a sad little sniffling cry issuing from his throat.

Then he looked down. Crouched at his feet was his tiny little son, the runt of the litter, looking up with adoring eyes at his daddy. It was as if Beethoven had suddenly been reminded of his responsibility as a parent. He stopped crying and his spine stiffened – he was pulling himself together. Beethoven leaned down and licked his little pup, reassuring him that everything would be all right.

Emily scooped up the runt and the three other puppies and dropped them into the cardboard box, pulling Ted's jacket over them, hiding them from view.

'OK,' Ted whispered. 'It's time to get out of here.'

Brother and sister tiptoed to the big heavy door and peeked out. 'The coast is clear,' said Emily. 'Let's go.'

They scurried out into the garage, just in time to hear Regina talking to Gus. They were waiting for the elevator that would take them back up to the ground floor of the apartment building.

'We're gonna be gone all summer, Gus,' said Regina. 'If my husband comes around looking for me or the dog, tell him to go to hell.'

'Yes, ma'am,' mumbled Gus. 'Have a nice time.' He was secretly relieved that this horrible woman would be off the premises and out of his hair for at least three months, possibly four – if he were lucky.

Regina was digging in her handbag. 'Darn!' she said. 'My sunglasses! I must have dropped them! . . . Gus, there's a red Lexus out front. Take the dog up there and tell Floyd to put this big mutt in the back seat.'

'Yes, ma'am.'

'Run!' hissed Ted.

They dashed across the garage and ran smack into Regina! She seemed to tower over them, and she glared down. Emily had never seen anyone quite so scary in her entire life. Her mouth dropped open. Instinctively, Ted shrank back from her. Beethoven growled and showed his teeth.

'Who are you?' snapped Regina.

Ted swallowed hard then stepped forward, holding the covered box out in front of him. He knew it was time for bold action – he just hoped the puppies kept still and quiet.

'Hello,' he said, managing a bright smile. 'Would you like to buy some chocolate bars?'

'Chocolate bars?' snorted Regina. 'What for?'

'To raise money for our school,' Ted replied.

'How much are they?' Regina asked impatiently.

This was the last thing Ted had planned on. He had never expected in a million years that a person like Regina would actually be interested in helping with a charity. Emily and Ted looked at each other in disbelief, not quite sure what to do or say next.

Finally, Emily spoke. 'They're eleven dollars each,' she said calmly.

'Eleven dollars? For a lousy candy bar? Forget it.' Regina pushed by them. 'Now, get your little brat butts out of here before I call building security.' Then she stopped and peered closely at Beethoven. 'Lot of St Bernards around all of a sudden. Strange . . .'

Ted gulped. 'OK. Thank you. Gotta be running along.' He grabbed Beethoven by the collar. 'Let's go.'

'Right,' said Emily. 'Thanks. Thanks a lot.'

A few minutes later, Ted and Emily were hurrying down the street when Regina's red sports car swept by them. Missy was crammed into the back seat with all of Regina's luggage, and her face was pushed up against the rear window. When she saw Beethoven, her eyes came alive and she began barking as if her heart would break.

In a flash, Beethoven bolted after the car, but Emily dived and caught him by the collar. Ted knelt down next to him and stroked his back.

'Don't worry, boy. She'll come back.'

'And right now we've got to take care of your children,' said Emily solemnly.

But Beethoven continued to watch the car as it drove away, following it down the road with big, sorrowful eyes. It was the saddest day of Beethoven's life.

Chapter 9

Ted and Emily had overcome one set of problems only to be confronted with another. They had managed to get the puppies away from Regina, and carrying them on the back of Ted's bicycle, they spirited them across town. *Now*, however, they faced the hurdle of getting them into their own house without anyone finding out – their dad, in particular!

They were not in luck. They thought that George Newton would be at his beloved factory, but they had forgotten that today was Sunday. Mr Newton had set himself the task of trimming every hedge and bush in the front and back gardens. Whether they needed it or not.

Luckily, Ted and Emily caught sight of their father before he saw them. They ducked behind a tree.

'Dad's on the lawn,' said Ted. 'What are we going to do?'

'*He* won't want puppies,' said Emily. '*He* didn't even want Beethoven.' Emily peeked around the tree and watched her father for a moment. 'He's trimming the hedge.'

Ted thought for a moment. 'You've got to distract him while I sneak around the back.'

'Distract him? How?'

'Ask him one of those questions where he ends up giving you a whole lecture.'

Emily nodded. 'Got it. Good idea.'

Beethoven, Ted and the puppies waited in their hiding-place while Emily stepped on to the lawn wondering just what she was going to ask her father. Then her face brightened – she thought of exactly the right thing! She started skipping across the lawn towards her dad.

George was trimming the hedge carefully, as if giving the bush a haircut. 'Hi, peanut,' he said to his daughter.

'Daddy,' Emily asked innocently, 'can I ask you a question?'

'Sure, sweetheart. What's on your mind?'

Emily smiled sweetly. 'Can you tell me where babies come from?'

George Newton winced slightly. He had hoped that this would be a question that Emily would, one day, address to her mother. But he knew he had to say *something* and not scare her away.

'Well . . . you see . . .' He snipped a couple of green branches off of the hedge while considering how to address this delicate subject.

'You see, sweetheart – every mommy has a teeny-weeny egg inside of her . . .'

Emily's eyes grew wide. 'An *egg*? Like an Easter egg, you mean?'

George shook his head. 'No. Not an Easter egg. *Smaller* than an Easter egg . . .'

'Like a robin's egg?' asked Emily.

'No . . . smaller . . .'

Emily watched as Ted sneaked across the lawn, hunched over the box of puppies, Beethoven trotting at his heels.

'How small?'

'More like a goldfish egg,' said George Newton. 'Only even smaller.'

'Smaller?' said Emily in disbelief.

Mr Newton nodded. 'Much smaller. And every so often that little, teeny, tiny egg floats down a little river in the mommy's body.'

Emily could hardly believe her ears. 'A river?'

George nodded. 'Absolutely. A teeny-tiny eenie-weeny little itty-bitty river . . .' With each word Mr Newton snipped another branch from the hedge.

Emily did not really listen to the next part of Mr Newton's little talk. She was watching Ted as he continued to creep across the lawn.

George Newton didn't realize that he had lost his daughter's attention.

'. . . and then out of the thousands and thousands of tiny tadpoles swimming around the little egg . . .'

Ted was just about to disappear through the cellar door. He waved to Emily and gave her the thumbs-up. He had made it past his father without getting caught.

Now the hard part, as far as Emily was concerned, was getting her father to end his little lecture. But he was warming to his subject.

'. . . *one* of them – the most determined little tadpole in the whole bunch, and the very best swimmer – winner of the Gold Medal in the tadpole Olympics . . .'

Emily was thoroughly confused – eggs, tadpoles, Olympics – none of this made much sense.

'The Olympics?' she asked.

'Well . . . they're not *exactly* Olympics.'

Emily didn't really want to hear any more. What she wanted to do was escape from her father and get inside and see Beethoven's puppies!

'Maybe we should talk about this when I'm a little older,' she suggested helpfully.

George was immensely relieved. 'You know, Emily, that's a very good idea.'

Ryce was sitting at the dressing table in her

bedroom, staring at herself in the mirror. She couldn't decide if she was pretty or not, nor could she figure out what on earth a cool, handsome guy like Taylor Devereaux could ever see in her.

Her reveries were interrupted by Ted, Emily and Beethoven creeping into her room. Ted touched his finger to his lips and motioned to his older sister.

Ryce was puzzled. 'What's up?'

'Just come with us,' said Emily in a whisper, 'and keep a look-out for Mom and Dad.'

'Especially Dad,' put in Ted.

Together all of the Newton children and their dog crept downstairs, through the kitchen and then down to the basement. Emily snapped on a flashlight and shone it on to a sleeping-bag bundled up in the corner of the cellar. Ted pulled the bag away and revealed their new-found treasures.

Ryce looked down in amazement. 'Puppies . . . Where did they come from?' she gasped in wonderment.

'They're Beethoven's,' said Emily. She grabbed the two who most closely resembled their father and showed them to Ryce. 'See?'

'They're so cute!'

Bending down, Ted pushed a bowl of milk into the middle of the makeshift pen, but the pups showed no interest in it at all. The children could see that Beethoven was very concerned about his little puppies. He came over and licked them reassuringly, trying to make them feel better. But he could tell they missed their mother. Beethoven was sad. *He* missed their mother too!

'How did this happen?' asked Ryce.

'The lady who owns their mother was going to drown them,' Emily explained. 'We just couldn't let that happen. So we brought them home with us.'

'Mom and Dad don't know,' said Ted. 'We're going to wait to tell them. Until Dad's in a good mood.'

'It'll have to be a *really* good mood,' said Ryce. 'The kind that comes along once in a hundred years.'

The puppies were whimpering and cowering in a corner. 'Little squeaks are OK,' he said to the dogs. 'Just don't bark until we figure out what we're going to do with you guys.'

'What are we going to call them?' asked Ted.

Ryce picked up the puppy closest to her. 'This one is a girl. Think of nice girl's name.'

'It's gotta be better than just nice,' protested Emily. 'Her father is Beethoven. He was a musician from a long time ago. She needs a musical name.'

They all thought for a moment.

'How about Dolly?' said Ryce. 'Like Dolly Parton.'

Emily nodded. 'That's good.' She picked up another puppy. 'This one is so fat ... He's Chubby!'

'Like Chubby Checker,' said Ryce.

'Who's that?'

Ryce frowned. 'I'm not sure. He was a singer, I think. I heard Mom and Dad talk about him. He was from when they were kids.'

'That was a long, long time ago,' said Emily.

Ted was examining another puppy. 'He looks like one of the Three Stooges. Let's call him Moe!'

His two sisters nodded in agreement. 'And one of them should have a real musical name,' said Ryce. 'Let's name the little one Tchaikovsky!'

'Who was that?' asked Ted.

Emily looked at her brother with disgust. 'Don't you know anything? He was in a band with Beethoven! Like, a hundred years ago!'

Chapter 10

It was a beautiful morning, even if it *was* a Monday. Mr Newton woke early – he was anxious to get back to his factory and get on with the business of creating Newton Sports Fresheners. However, he did take time that morning to try and relax a little, to sip his coffee and savour the day. Still wearing his dressing-gown, Mr Newton wandered out on to the porch of his house, a steaming mug of coffee in his hand. He took a deep breath of the fresh air and exhaled heavily, glad to be alive.

Then he saw Tommy the paperboy furiously pedalling his bike towards the Newton house.

'Hey, Mr Newton!' Tommy shouted, slightly out of breath. 'It's the ninth inning. The count is full . . .'

Somewhat reluctantly, George Newton put his coffee mug well out of the line of fire and cautiously assumed the crouch of a baseball catcher.

'OK, Tommy,' shouted Mr Newton. 'Straight down the pipe. Nothing but smoke . . .'

'You got it!' Tommy pulled a paper from his bag and whipped it straight at George. For a moment or two, it looked as if the paper was going to hit its mark. Then, like a major league curveball gone wrong, the newspaper arched upwards and slammed into a hanging pot of geraniums just above Mr Newton's head. In a second, a couple of pounds of heavily fertilized dirt poured on to George's head.

It looked as if it was going to be that same old lousy Monday after all . . .

Things weren't going so well down in the basement either. The puppies were pining for Missy, and they absolutely refused to eat. Ryce, Ted and Emily were not experts in child rearing, but they knew that Beethoven's little offspring had to eat if they were to survive. But they wouldn't.

Ted had a brimming bowl of milk in his hands, and Emily held one of the puppies up to it, hoping to see a little pink tongue dart out and lap it up. But the milk went untouched.

Emily had to blink back her tears. 'C'mon, Dolly – *please* take a sip.'

But the tiny puppy turned her head away from the milk. Emily and Ted exchanged anxious looks and wondered what they could do to make the puppies take nourishment.

A few feet away, Ryce was talking on a portable phone. She had done the sensible thing and called the veterinarian who looked after Beethoven.

'Yes, Doctor, the puppies are *very* young,' said Ryce. 'And their mother has gone, and they won't drink milk from a bowl or anything . . .' Ryce glanced at the puppies, who were completely ignoring Ted's dish of milk.

'Uh – huh . . .' said Ryce. 'We have to get something called milk replacement powder and feed them with an eyedropper. I understand. Thank you . . .' Ryce hung up and looked at her brother and sister. 'Well, now we know.'

'If we get some of that stuff they'll eat,' said Ted. 'That's great!'

'There's a problem,' said Ryce.

'What problem?' asked Emily.

'They have to be fed around the clock. Six to eight times a day – every day.'

'How are we going to do that?' said Emily. 'We have to sleep and go to school . . .'

'The vet said it's only for a few days, then we mix the stuff with baby food and get them to lick if off our fingers. Then, at some point if we're lucky, they'll start eating from a bowl by themselves.'

Ted shook his head. 'I just don't see how we're going to feed them six times a day on school days.'

'We'll just have to try,' said Ryce with a shrug. 'We'll work it out.'

Suddenly, the cellar door opened. 'Kids?' George Newton called from the top of the stairs. 'What on earth are you doing down there?'

The three Newton children leapt into action, placing the puppies back in their makeshift pen and covering them up with the sleeping-bag.

George started down the stairs. 'Is someone down there?'

Emily pushed Beethoven forward. 'You know what to do,' she whispered. 'Go!'

Beethoven took off like a shot, racing up the stairs, barrelling towards George Newton like a furry missile.

'Beethoven!' yelled George. 'No!'

The kids winced as they heard the impact of dog on man followed seconds later by the crash of pots and pans as Beethoven slammed George into the kitchen.

George scrambled to his feet. 'Beethoven! Have you gone crazy?'

Beethoven did, in fact, appear to have lost his mind. Gently but relentlessly he pushed George towards the front door of the house, like a sheepdog herding a flock.

'OK,' said George. 'Outside. No, not *me* outside. *You* outside!'

But Beethoven refused to be thwarted, steadily pushing Mr Newton out of the front door. George wrapped his hands around one of the banisters and held on. 'Alice! Help!'

Beethoven forced George Newton out of the front door, then nudged it closed with his nose. The door clicked shut and locked, leaving Mr Newton stranded outside.

He pounded hard on the door. 'Alice! Alice, open up!' He hated Mondays!

Chapter 11

Somehow, Mr Newton managed to get through the day, but by that evening he was still working – in fact, he almost always brought work home with him these days. The sports freshener business was a lot more complicated than he had thought it would be. Every detail had to be attended to, right down to the advertising.

Alice watched her husband as he sat at a table trying to figure out some copy for the commercials he planned to produce for his new product. She picked up one of the fresheners, the one shaped like a hockey player, and sniffed it.

'What's the hockey player made of?'

George hardly looked up from his work. 'Mahogany vanilla. And if you think that's good, wait until you smell the one shaped like a sumo wrestler.'

'Can't wait,' said Alice.

'OK,' said Mr Newton. 'I need a word that rhymes with "hypersensitive". It's for the television ad.'

Alice Newton frowned. 'I don't think there is one. Does it have to be hypersensitive?'

This was the kind of thing that made George

frustrated, when members of his own family didn't understand his brave new air freshener vision.

'Alice, *please*,' he said sharply. 'Our customers think of themselves as hypersensitive people.'

'They do?'

'Yes, they do. Every day they're at the mercy of irritating odours. I want to give these people a chance to fight back against those odours. When I say "Throw in a Newton", it's like saying "Throw in a hand grenade" or "Throw in an atomic bomb".'

Alice looked at her husband as if he was were crazy. 'Honey, I think you're working too hard. You need to take a break and get your perspective back.'

Mr Newton put down his pen. 'You think so?'

Alice Newton nodded. 'I know so. Go spend some time with the kids. Have some fun. When you come back, we'll talk about the ad.'

George nodded. 'You're right. We've got great kids . . .' He stood up and started out of the room. 'I'm going to go spend some time with my kids.'

'You do that, honey,' said Alice.

George Newton stepped into the hallway. 'Kids?'

In Ryce's room, the three children – and

Beethoven – froze when they heard Mr Newton's voice. There were calendars and schedules scattered all over Ryce's bed - but worse than that, one of the puppies was sitting in Emily's lap.

'Kids?' called Mr Newton. 'Where are you?'

'Uh . . . We're in Ryce's room,' said Ted.

'Good!' shouted George Newton. 'I'll be right there.'

Those were exactly the words the children feared most! The three kids jumped into action. Emily stuffed the puppy under the bed, and Ryce and Ted jammed the papers into the drawers of Ryce's desk.

By the time Mr Newton pushed open the bedroom door, the three kids were sprawled on the bed, each of them staring intently at a Monopoly board. If you didn't know better, you would have sworn that the kids had been playing a board game for hours.

George looked lovingly at his children, and his children looked back as if they were as innocent as little angels.

In unison, Ryce, Ted and Emily said: 'Hi, Daddy!'

'Hello,' said Mr Newton.

'Did we forget to do something?' asked Ryce.

George Newton shook his head. 'No.'

'Uh . . . said Ted. 'Did you want to speak to us about something?'

'No. Hey, you playing Monopoly? Can I play? I'd like to be the milk bottle.'

The children shifted uncomfortably and didn't exactly make their father feel welcome.

'Well,' said Ryce reluctantly, 'we're kind of close to the end of the game, Dad.'

George refused to be put off by the cold shoulder. 'Well, maybe I could be banker.'

Suddenly, Chubby the puppy popped out from under the bed and wandered around a few inches behind George Newton's left foot. Emily almost gasped!

'What's the matter, honey?' George asked.

'Emily's the banker,' said Ted quickly.

'It improves my maths skills,' said Emily.

'Oh,' said George. 'OK. I didn't mean to take your job away from you . . . But the next time you're going to play, call me, OK?'

Ryce could hardly take her eyes off Chubby, who was now sniffing at Mr Newton's heels.

'OK, Dad.'

All three children stared at him with fixed, rigid smiles. George began to feel distinctly uncomfortable and he stared back at them for a moment. Then he looked down – just as Chubby went back under the bed! If Mr Newton had glanced down just a split second sooner, he would have seen the fat little puppy staring up at him.

'OK ...' said Mr Newton uncomfortably. 'I'll run along and let you finish your game.' There was a sad little smile on George's face as he left the room. He wasn't welcome, he decided, because he was working too hard, spending too much time at the factory. If he wasn't careful, he'd lose his kids altogether ...

The instant their father was gone, the kids sprang back into action.

'I told you not to bring him upstairs, Emily,' said Ted, reaching for the schedules.

'What could I do? He was lonely.'

'You just wanted to play with him, that's all.'

'That too,' Emily admitted.

'C'mon,' said Ryce. 'Let's get serious here.' She consulted her school timetable. 'Mondays and Wednesday I have free periods in the morning.'

Ted nodded. 'Then Emily and I can do the lunch-hour while Mom's helping Dad at the office.'

'Right,' said Ryce. 'Any chance you can get home and back during breaktime?'

Ted shook his head emphatically. 'Morning break is too short. We can make it home in the afternoons. If we run both ways.'

Ryce frowned and consulted her schedule. 'Then the real problems are Tuesday, Thursday and Friday mornings ...'

'What are we going to do?' said Emily.

'I'll figure something out,' said Ryce.

Ryce was not a sneaky kid, but she knew how to pull a fast one when in an emergency. The first thing she did when she got to school next morning was get her friend Michelle to take down a note that Ryce dictated.

'I can't believe I'm doing this,' said Michelle, half hiding inside her locker as she wrote. 'I think forgery is some kind of crime.'

'Don't worry about it,' said Ryce. 'Just write what I tell you.' She cleared her throat. 'Dear Mrs Anderson. Please excuse Ryce from chemistry class on Tuesday, Thursday and Friday mornings.'

'Boy, you must really hate chemistry.'

'Now . . . Why aren't I going to chemistry class? . . .' She thought for a moment, then snapped her fingers. 'Got it! Ryce cannot attend on these mornings because she has a doctor's appointment to get allergy shots . . .' Ryce's voice trailed off suddenly.

'Yeah?' said Michelle. 'How does the letter end?' Then she looked up and saw what Ryce was looking at.

Down the corridor, Ryce had caught sight of Taylor standing in front of his locker. He was talking and laughing – flirting – with a very pretty teenage girl. She was in a higher class than Ryce and looked a lot more grown-up. The girl laughed and brushed the hair out of Taylor's eyes.

Ryce felt a stab of jealousy, but she fought it and tried to finish dictating the letter.

'Just sign it,' said Ryce quietly. 'Yours truly, George M. Newton . . .'

Michelle finished writing the letter and then did her best to make her friend feel better. She cast a scornful glance at the girl that had caught Taylor's fancy. 'I mean,' said Michelle, 'I can see right through her blouse. Like, that's a total accident, I'm sure.'

Ryce turned away. 'C'mon,' she said. 'Let's go to class.'

'She's nothing, Ryce. Don't worry about her,' said Michelle soothingly.

But Ryce just shrugged. She wasn't in the mood to be cheered up.

Chapter 12

The next few days passed in a blur for the Newton children as they raced back and forth between school and home to feed the puppies still hidden in their basement. It was not easy to dash out of class, ride their bikes home and then begin the lengthy process of getting the puppies to accept the food. On top of this, Ryce, Ted and Emily had to take care that no teachers saw them leaving the school grounds and that they didn't run into their mother or father when they did get home.

When they weren't dashing out of school to do the feedings, they were waking up in the dead of night and creeping down to the basement to give the pups their baby food. And because they were missing so much sleep at night, their hectic days were harder and harder. Ted found it impossible to get through gym class, and once or twice Ryce actually dozed off in the middle of algebra.

However, there was one good thing about all this exhausting activity. The puppies were eating! Every day they became stronger and stronger, friskier and healthier. The kids were worn out from all their hard work, but one look at the four puppies playing and frolicking, wrestling and tumbling over their fat little legs and they realized that all their sacrifice had been well worth it. Beethoven, too, looked like the proud father, and they could tell by the look in his eyes that he appreciated all that they had done to keep his children alive.

None the less, after a full week of this tiring routine, all three children were completely worn out – a fact that Mrs Newton did not fail to notice.

One night, before dinner, Ted, Ryce and Emily were sitting in the family room trying to keep their eyes open as they watched TV when Mrs Newton came into the room. She looked at her children as they yawned, and she wagged a finger at them.

'I can tell you one thing,' she said sternly. 'It's going to be early to bed for you three tonight!'

It was never an easy task to get her kids into bed, but if she expected an argument from them on this score, she didn't get one that night.

Ted, Ryce and Emily just nodded sleepily. 'OK, Mom,' said Ryce, speaking for all of them.

Just then the phone rang. Usually there was a scramble for the phone too, but this evening not one of the children lifted a finger to answer it.

'Hello,' said Alice.

'Mrs Newton?' It was a woman's voice.

'Yes?'

'Mrs Newton, this is Linda Anderson. I teach Ryce chemistry. And I was just calling to make sure if she's all right.'

'Why?' Alice asked, glancing over at Ryce as she spoke. 'Did something happen?'

'No,' said Mrs Anderson. 'It's just that with so little school left before the summer vacation, I'm a little concerned with her missing so many classes. I'm worried that she might have a problem catching up when she comes back to school after getting that course of allergy shots.'

'Allergy shots?' said Mrs Newton. '*What* allergy shots?'

Suddenly, at the sound of those two words, Ryce was wide awake and she swallowed hard. 'Ooops,' she said.

Mrs Newton put down the phone and snapped her fingers at Emily and Ted. 'You two. Hit the road. I need to talk to your sister here.'

'But, Mom –' said Ted.

'No buts, mister. Scram.'

The boy and girl walked slowly out of the room as Mrs Newton settled herself on the couch next to her oldest daughter. She looked very serious. Ryce looked very worried.

'Have you been skipping school to spend time with boys?' Mrs Newton asked.

Ryce shook her head. 'No.'

'Are you taking drugs?'

'No,' said Ryce. Drugs weren't for her. And she knew they never would be.

'Is . . . is somebody you know pregnant?'

'No,' said Ryce firmly.

'Then why are you cutting classes?'

Ryce looked down, unable to meet her mother's steady gaze. 'I can't tell you.'

Alice Newton didn't get angry with her daughter. In fact, she could tell that Ryce's inability to confide in her mother was causing her pain.

She took her daughter's hand and stroked it. 'Honey, please,' she said softly. 'We've always talked about things, haven't we?'

'Uh-huh,' Ryce admitted.

'Then don't stop now,' said Alice, 'right when we really need to be honest with each other.'

Ryce looked up and met her mother's earnest gaze. She took a deep breath, as if it would give her courage. 'Ted and Emily and I have been hiding four puppies in the basement.'

'Puppies?' said Alice. Suddenly, she felt a great relief flooding through her. All this secrecy had been about something as innocent as a litter of puppies? The possibilities had been so much worse that she almost wanted to laugh from relief.

Instead, she did her best to keep up a stern Mom face. 'I don't understand. Why weren't you in school? Why did you have to make up stories?'

'I had to cut class a couple of times, Mom,' said Ryce quickly. 'The puppies were too little to eat from a bowl so we had to feed them six times a day to keep them alive. They just started eating by themselves today.'

Suddenly, they heard the front door of the house open. 'I'm ho-ome!' shouted George Newton.

'Uh-oh,' said Alice. Puppies were not nearly as bad as drugs or any of the other things she had imagined, but she wasn't sure just how her husband would take it. 'Let's keep this a secret from Dad,' said Alice. 'Just for a little while.'

Chapter 13

The kids may have been worn out, but George Newton was crackling with energy. His new factory equipment was installed and running at full speed, the publicity machine was in high gear and Mr Newton figured he could smell a winner. In fact, he said that, 'smell a winner', expecting gales of laughter from his family. The best he could get, though, was some tired, but happy, smiles from his three children. The whole family was gathered at the dinner table, but the kids were almost asleep in their dinner plates.

Nevertheless, he kept talking, bubbling with enthusiasm for his new product.

'The buyer from Wal-Mart called. Just to say hello. That means the buzz is starting. They know that we're coming out with something hot.'

'That's great, dear,' said Alice.

'And' – Mr Newton smiled and paused dramatically, like a magician about to pull something from his top hat – 'on another front – kids, your father has found the perfect weekend getaway for a family with a limited cash flow.'

Alice Newton frowned, but Mr Newton waved

away her concerns. 'This we can afford. Fred Serbiak – the man who supplies our Velcro – has a cottage in the mountains that he's been inviting us to go to for years.'

'We're going on vacation with someone else?' asked Ted.

'No,' George explained patiently. 'Fred's family won't go up there until after the Fourth of July. So, as soon as school ends, we are going to go up there and spend four fun-filled days at Fred Serbiak's mountain getaway. Absolutely free!'

Ryce was very interested in this news. Taylor Devereaux's family had a place up in the mountains. But Ryce wasn't sure if she was happy or sad about it.

'Is that near the place we rented last summer?' she asked as she toyed with her salad.

George was delighted to have got some kind of reaction from his children. 'As a matter of fact it is,' he said, beaming happily. 'Of course, Fred wasn't too happy about us having a dog, but I assured him that our little guy would not be a problem.' George was in such a good mood that night that it even extended to Beethoven.

Mr Newton bent down and ruffled Beethoven's fur. 'Isn't that right, you little chihuahua you?'

The Beethoven we know and love

How things used to be – George Newton and Beethoven

But things change. Beethoven meets Missy

Beethoven says 'hello' to Missy

Beethoven gets lovesick

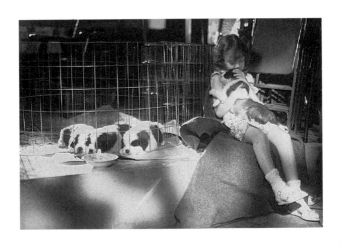

Puppies arrive on the scene

Beethoven looks on ...

... whilst the kids play with the puppies

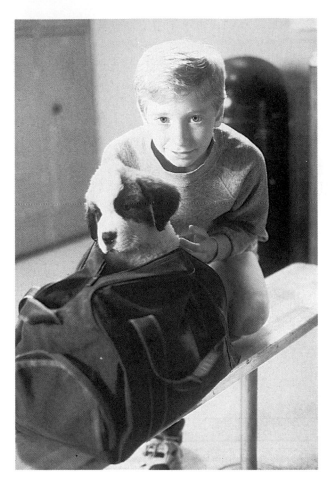

Ted puts a puppy in a grip

Mr Newton gets to grip with two puppies

Trouble on the mountain

The whole family reunited

Beethoven was delighted that George Newton was being nice to him, and he barked happily!

Then, from downstairs in the basement, there was an answering bark. A high-pitched little yip from one of the puppies.

All of the kids froze, but Ted was thinking fast. He faked a great big sneeze and hoped that it covered up the noise of the little bark from downstairs.

'Bless you, Ted,' said George Newton. 'Just think about this vacation, kids! No phone, no bills, no worries. No nothing. Just peace.'

But there was another little bark from the basement. This time, Ryce did her best to distract her father from the sound by dragging her chair across the floor. She stood up.

'I think I'll run a quick load through the dishwasher,' she said, gathering up the dinner plates.

George Newton looked puzzled. 'I appreciate your enthusiasm, but isn't it kind of customary to run the dishwasher *after* the meal?'

Ryce shrugged and sat down again. 'I guess so.'

Mr Newton turned his attention back to his plate of food, eating heartily. 'Now, I don't know about you guys, but I have been working my buns off. And I need a little vacation. I *need* a –'

There was another bark from downstairs, a louder one this time. There was no mistaking it – and everyone heard it loud and clear.

'. . . a few days away . . .' He looked down to make sure that Beethoven was still seated at his feet. He was. But that didn't stop Beethoven from trying to give out the tiniest, daintiest little bark he could in the hope that Mr Newton would think *he* had made the faint little bark.

But it was no good. All four of the puppies were barking now, and no one could do anything about it.

George put down his fork. 'Are those sounds outside or are they coming from the basement?'

All three kids plus Alice spoke at once, in perfect unison:

'Outside!'

Slowly, George got up from his place. 'No, I think it's coming from inside. I think there's some kind of animal in our basement . . .' Stealthily, he made his way to the door. 'Everybody stay here,' he ordered. 'I'm going to go find out what's going on down there.'

The family looked on nervously as George started down the basement stairs. He snapped the light switch, but the light did not turn on. 'The light-bulb seems to have burnt out. Do we have any extra light-bulbs?'

All three kids jumped to their feet – anything to delay their father from going down there.

'I'll get 'em!' said Ted.

'No, me!' said Ryce.

'I'll do it,' said Emily.

'You're too short!' insisted Ted.

'It'll take longer,' replied Emily.

'There's no need,' said Mr Newton. 'Everybody sit down. I found a flashlight.' He snapped it on and continued down the stairs.

The kids returned to their supper, picking at their food listlessly. There was a long moment of silence, then from the basement came a scream.

'Aaaaaaaaah!' wailed Mr Newton as if he had seen a horrible monster – but this was much worse. '*Puppies!*'

Chapter 14

It took a little while for George Newton to calm down, but eventually Alice managed to get him back upstairs and more or less composed. However, once his anger burnt off, the Newton children could tell that their father was determined to get rid of the puppies. In a way, they would have preferred it if he had ranted and raved and waved his arms and pounded his fist. Instead, he was quiet and collected and absolutely firm.

Ted and Emily told the story of how they had saved the puppies, hoping that the sad tale would melt their father's hard heart.

'. . . then the lady told the janitor to come back when she had gone and drown them,' said Ted.

'But they were Beethoven's too,' put in Emily.

'So rather than let them die, we brought them home.' Ted shrugged his shoulders. 'What else could we do, Dad? We couldn't let some man drown Beethoven's children.'

George frowned and slowly shook his head.

'Can we keep them?' asked Emily.

'No,' said George firmly. 'It's out of the question.'

'When they're older,' said Ted solemnly, 'we'll find homes for them. That's a promise.'

George Newton shook his head again. 'No. Absolutely not.'

A heavy silence hung over the table, and George could feel the eyes of his entire family on him.

'George –' began Alice.

'No!' said George. 'Is it so hard to understand? One little word. *No!*'

'Why not?' his wife challenged. 'Just give us one good reason.'

'One reason?' said George. 'I'll give you more than one. I'll give you five.'

'Five?' said Ted.

'That's right. This isn't *one* dog. This is *five* dogs.'

'Four are *little* dogs,' said Emily.

'They're little dogs now,' Mr Newton shot back, 'and although they look harmless, very soon they're going to turn into *monster* dogs. Four more Beethovens! Can you imagine that?'

Emily's eyes were bright. *She* couldn't imagine anything better than five Beethovens!

'They'll destroy our house!' insisted Mr Newton. 'They'll wreck the Serbiaks' cottage. And they'll drive us out of our minds. So believe me when I tell you – hygienically, emotionally and financially, we cannot afford these dogs!'

Emily decided to attack on the financial front. 'I'll use my allowance to pay for their food.'

'No,' said George, 'it's insanity.'

Alice gave her husband her absolutely most appealing, pleading look.

But George Newton was immune. 'You can look at me all you want, but the answer is still no. Now, could we please just forget about it?'

Of course, no one could forget about it. It was Ryce's turn to try and change her father's mind. By the look on her face, it was apparent that she had a plan, a carefully worked-out argument to use on her father.

'They would be a lot of trouble, wouldn't they?' she asked quietly.

George Newton rolled his eyes. 'Untrained St Bernard puppies? Of course! They would be an enormous amount of trouble. They would be trouble like we couldn't even begin to imagine.'

Ryce was ready with the next phase of her argument, but it was plain that her father had no idea that she had laid a deadly trap for him.

'Was I a lot of trouble when I was a baby?'

George Newton replied reluctantly. 'Well . . . yeah. I suppose so.'

'Well,' asked Ryce, 'what about when there were three of us. That was probably a lot harder, wasn't it?'

George nodded. '*That* was beyond trouble . . .' He turned to his wife. 'Do you remember how we were on the verge of losing our minds?'

'Oh, yes. Absolutely!' Alice nodded vigorously. She had already guessed where Ryce was going with this argument, and she suspected that it just might work.

'Would you rather have had less trouble and just stopped after you had me?' Ryce asked innocently. She knew the answer already, of course.

'No,' said George. 'Of course not. But you're our children. These are *dogs*.'

'They're *our* children,' insisted Ryce.

But Mr Newton refused to be swayed. 'The answer is no. I will *not* be responsible for five dogs.'

Ryce lost her cool. 'You don't *have* to be responsible! *We've* already been responsible. We've gone through hell for these puppies. And if being this responsible means we lose them now, then I hate responsibility.' Ryce was leaning forward now, tears in her eyes. 'We kept them *alive*, Daddy! Like Mom and you kept *us* alive.' Ryce threw herself back in the chair and folded her arms across her chest. 'And you're not going to take them away from us!'

George had never seen his daughter quite so intense. He was amazed at the strength of her emotion – even Alice was astounded that she could get so worked up.

Ryce took a deep breath and tried to calm herself down. 'If we keep them,' she said quietly, 'maybe when they're bigger we'll find homes for them. But it should be a situation the whole family can live with.'

George Newton looked from Ryce to Ted and finally to Emily. The children stared back at him, total and complete commitment on their faces. Suddenly, his three kids looked older, more capable and confident. He rested his head on his hands and sighed heavily, knowing that he had to give in.

'OK . . .'

Suddenly, all three kids were on their feet cheering and yelling. Beethoven barked happily! Ted, Ryce and Emily threw their arms around their father and smothered him in hugs.

'It's only for a little while,' he said, raising his voice to make himself heard above their screams of delight.

'Thank you, Daddy!' said Ryce. 'I'm sorry I shouted at you!'

'C'mon,' shouted Emily. 'Let's take the puppies outside right now!'

The children raced out of the dining-room. The instant they were gone, Beethoven approached Mr Newton and tenderly licked his owner's hand. Then the big dog bounded after the children.

Sadly, George looked to his wife. 'What else could I do? They would have been heartbroken if –'

'You did absolutely the right thing, George,' said Alice, looking at her husband with deep affection. 'They meant what they said. They'll be able to handle it. The kids will find a way. And if they need a little help . . .'

Mr Newton sighed again. 'Then we'll have to give it to them, I suppose . . . *Now* maybe we can have a few moments of peace – before things get really crazy around here . . .'

Chapter 15

Mr Newton's period of peace did not last long. In a matter of days Tchaikovsky, Chubby, Dolly and Moe had taken over the whole Newton house. Puppies love to chew, and the first thing they decided to chew on was Mr Newton's slippers.

So George decided that if you couldn't beat 'em you should join 'em. He had a theory that the puppies were so destructive because they had too much energy, so Mr Newton decided that he would take the puppies on his daily two-mile run. He was right about the energy levels of the puppies, but he didn't count on the fact that he would never be able to keep up with them. Before he had run a block or two, the puppies, on their leashes, were pulling him down the street and George was absolutely exhausted!

The puppies were incredibly mischievous – particularly Tchaikovsky. He had gone from the runt of the litter to being the most active of all of them. He loved to go out and explore in the street.

But Ted, Ryce and Emily didn't like it when the puppies escaped. It was very dangerous. One day, Tchaikovsky got loose from the puppy pen that Mr Newton had built in the back garden and went racing into the street. Like a shot, the kids went racing after him, but Tchaikovsky dived for cover under a parked car.

None of the kids could reach the little furball, so George had to reach under to get him. But just as he flattened himself on the road to get the puppy, a street-cleaning truck happened to come down the street spraying water. The water washed Tchaikovsky to the safety of the kerb, where Emily grabbed him. But Mr Newton got soaked to the skin!

Beethoven had passed more than his good looks on to his sons and daughters – like their father, the four puppies loved George Newton to pieces! At night, when all the kids were finally in bed, Mr Newton settled down on the couch to watch the late news on TV. He hardly ever saw it, though, because he was usually so tired that he fell asleep before the programme started.

The instant his eyes closed, the four little pups crept up on the couch, one by one, until Mr Newton was completely covered by four furry puppies.

For the longest time, Mr Newton couldn't figure out how the puppies escaped from their pen. Every morning George would carefully load the puppies into it, Beethoven standing by to round up any of the pups that might wander off. Then, the instant Mr Newton left for work, Beethoven would creep to the enclosure and let them out! Mr Newton suspected that his children let them out – never suspecting that Beethoven was getting pretty good at opening doors!

The children loved to play with the little dogs. Emily had her own special game. She would sneak one of the puppies into the upstairs bathroom and, using a comb and a jar of Vaseline, she would design new hairstyles for her little friends. Her favourite was a spiky Mohican style for Chubby! And he didn't seem to mind either.

George was a great believer in family togetherness. He tried to get Alice and all the children together for a nice family photograph. Of course, as far as Ted, Emily and Ryce were concerned, Beethoven and all four puppies were full members of the Newton clan, and they insisted that all the dogs be included in the picture.

Mr Newton set his camera on automatic then hurried back to kneel on the lawn in the middle of his human and canine family. Beethoven and his brood were obediently standing to attention looking at the camera – but none of them could resist the temptation when a neighbour's cat ran by. Ignoring the camera, all five dogs took off after the cat, throwing the whole picture into chaos!

Ted tried to teach the puppies to fetch. He would throw a stick as far as he could, and all the puppies would take off after it. Usually, one of the puppies would come back with the stick - or *some* stick - in its mouth, but the rest of them would retrieve anything they could get their little mouths on! Sometimes it was a piece of the neighbour's laundry, or maybe a fresh steak from yet another neighbour's barbecue. Ted was never sure what they would come back with!

The puppies were curious about everything and had practically no fear about anything. They had the run of the house, of course, and they went snooping everywhere. They were particularly fascinated by the bathroom.

One day, Dolly and Moe ventured to the upstairs bathroom. While Moe watched, Dolly clambered up on to the toilet seat and bent over trying to reach the water in the bowl. But her little claws couldn't hold on the slippery smooth surface of the seat, and suddenly she tumbled into the water with a big splash!

Moe had never see anyone fall in water before and it scared him. He started barking as loud as he could, hoping that someone would come quick and rescue his sister. A second later, George

Newton dashed into the bathroom and without thinking about it, thrust his arm deep into the toilet water to recover the struggling and scared little pup! Dolly and Moe were delighted, but Mr Newton had wet his shirtsleeve all the way up to his shoulder!

Of course, there were benefits to having the puppies around the house – even Mr Newton had to admit that. One evening, Alice and her husband discovered all three of their children asleep on the floor of the family room, and all four puppies were cuddled with them, Beethoven standing guard over his whole family.

Mr and Mrs Newton had never seen anything so cute in their entire lives. It was at times like these that George felt really good about letting the puppies stay.

He wondered, though, what he was going to do when the time came for the puppies to go. He was afraid that he would end up breaking his children's hearts. And one thing was for sure, the puppies couldn't stay for ever . . .

Chapter 16

Finally, the big day arrived. School was over, and it was time for the Newtons to take off on their holidays to the mountains. The whole family was up early, and they bustled about loading up the station wagon. The car was heaped with suitcases and sleeping-bags, as well as a portable stereo, dolls, baskets of food, snacks, fishing and swimming gear, boxes of board games, books, magazines and tapes. By the time the car was packed, it looked as if the Newtons were going away for a month, not for just an extended weekend!

The last things to be loaded on board were the puppies. Ryce and Emily were putting them in the backseat while Alice watched them.

'And have they done all their little doodie pee pee kaka?' she asked.

Emily nodded. 'Yup. I'm a witness.'

George came up to his wife and put an arm around Alice's shoulders. Proudly, he examined his fully packed car and his happy family.

'I love this,' he said. 'The gang of us just hitting the road. It's just great. You know, already I feel like a totally different person.'

'Who have you become?' Alice asked with a laugh. 'Anyone I know?'

George Newton thought for a moment. 'I have become Mister Fun!' he announced. 'Children, children everywhere! Mister Fun says get in the car!'

'OK, Mister Fun!' yelled the Newton children, clambering into the car.

'You too, large hairy dog!' Mr Newton called out to Beethoven.

With a single bound, Beethoven leapt into the rear of the station wagon, his tail thumping happily on the floor, raising clouds of dust.

Mr Newton slammed the station-wagon doors. 'Attention, all Newtons!' he announced. 'Mister Fun says it's time to rock!'

With the car radio tuned to an oldies station, George and Alice Newton sang along with the tunes. The kids were amazed that their parents knew all the words to ancient songs like 'Duke of Earl', 'Leader of the Pack', 'Chapel of Love' and a ditty mysteriously named 'Do-Wah Diddy Diddy (Dum-Diddy-Doo)'.

Emily fell asleep almost immediately with Chubby in her lap. Ted wore a Walkman (mostly to drown out his father's singing) and read a Spiderman comic while Tchaikovsky and Dolly snuggled against him. Ryce had Moe in her lap, and she stroked his head absentmindedly as she looked out of the window, lost in a daydream.

The journey passed quickly. Before long, they had left the main highway and were climbing up a twisting mountain road that led through a forest of tall, stately pine trees. They were pretty high up in the hills, and the air smelled fresh and clean and the sunlight was bright and clear. George took a deep breath and wished that they were staying longer.

Half-way around a bend they passed a sign: Lake MacDonald $\frac{1}{2}$ mile. A smaller sign near by read: Copper Mountain Road – AAA Kennels – Next right . . .

'Lake MacDonald,' Mr Newton said. 'Here we come!'

All the kids were leaning forward in the back seat, craning their necks to catch the first glimpse of Lake MacDonald. They came around a tight bend, and all of a sudden there it was! Looking down from the high mountain road, they could see the beautiful lake, a great sweep of shining blue water, nestled at the foot of a tall, craggy mountain. Lining the shore of the lake were a dozen or two cottages – one of them belonging to Fred Serbiak. Most of the cottages were rather modest, simple cabins meant to be occupied for a couple of weeks a year. But there were one or two rather grand summer homes, large houses with landscaped lawns and swimming pools and tennis courts. On the far side of the lake was the little village.

'It's all so pretty!' exclaimed Ryce. 'It seems ever prettier than last year!'

A few minutes later the Newtons' car rolled to a stop in front of their cottage, and immediately kids and dogs started pouring out!

Ted went running towards the water. 'Look! There's a dock! And a rowing boat!'

The puppies were not so interested in the water or the dock, but they had picked up the scent of a chipmunk, and so the four little dogs were running around in four different directions trying to find it!

George and Alice stepped up to the porch and looked out over the crystal-clear lake. The view was lovely, and suddenly Alice felt relaxed and peaceful. She put her head on her husband's shoulder, and he held her close.

'This was a good idea, Mister Fun,' she whispered.

Chapter 17

Of course, even in a pretty, charming place like Lake MacDonald there are places that aren't very nice. The Newton family didn't know it yet, but on the other side of the lake was the very cottage that Regina and Floyd had rented. It was a gloomy place in a dark hollow at the base of Copper Mountain, not a sunny and open place like the Newtons' cottage.

But neither Regina nor Floyd were nature lovers. As far as they were concerned it was just a place to lie low long enough for Mr Brillo to *really* yearn for Missy.

They had been up there for almost a month now, and Mr Brillo had called Regina. He was ready to give up and pay anything he had in order to get his dog back.

Regina was delighted to get his call. 'Yes, Brillo,' she said. 'The extra million bucks gets you an uncontested divorce and your little doggie back . . .'

'You better be serious about this, Regina,' said Mr Brillo. 'Because I'm not kidding around.'

'Don't worry about it,' she said. 'You can

have her as soon as we sign the papers.'

'When?' demanded Mr Brillo.

'The day after tomorrow. Sunday. You come up here. I'll have my lawyer send you directions ... Bye.' Feeling very pleased with herself, Regina hung up the phone. But then there was a crash from the living-room followed by the sound of something breaking. Suddenly, Regina's smile turned to a frown.

Floyd and Regina dashed into the living-room. A glass sculpture lay smashed on the floor, next to an overturned pedestal. Missy had knocked it over by accident, and she was cowering in the corner, knowing that Regina was going to get very angry with her.

'You stupid, stupid animal!' Regina screamed. She grabbed the thing nearest to her − a box of tissus − and threw it at Missy, the cardboard container hitting her on the side of the head. Missy whimpered and cringed, trying to squeeze herself into a smaller target.

'I've had it with you!' screamed Regina.

'Yeah,' said Floyd. 'What a dumb animal!'

'Three more days I have to live with this moronic animal and I'll tell you this − she's not going to do any more damage to this place.' Regina grabbed a telephone-book and scrabbled through the thin pages frantically. 'Aha! Kennels!

116

There's one just outside of town!' She grabbed the phone and dialled quickly. A moment later an elderly woman answered. 'Triple A Kennels!'

'Yeah? Hello? I want to buy a cage for a St Bernard and I need it fast.'

'A St Bernard? That would be a pretty big cage,' said the old lady.

'Do you have one or not?' asked Regina impatiently.

'Yes,' said the old lady slowly. 'It's big enough. Cost you eight hundred dollars.'

'That's too much,' snapped Regina. 'I'm a little short of cash right now. Have you got anything else?'

'I've got all kinds of cages, lady, and they're all cheaper. But they're all a lot smaller too.'

Regina glowered at Missy, who shrank back from her cold glance. 'Don't worry about it. She'll get used to it . . .'

The small lakeside village was a perfect little country town. There were only a couple of streets and not many shops besides a big old general store, the food market and the petrol station. On the town green in front of the small town hall some of the local residents were tossing horseshoes.

The whole Newton family, Beethoven and the

puppies included, walked into town, eager to explore their new neighbourhood.

'Don't you just love places like this?' George looked around him. 'I mean, look at those people playing horseshoes. They're so . . . *real*.'

Alice nodded. 'And equally real is the fact that we have nothing for dinner. OK, kids, who wants to come on food patrol with me?'

'I do,' said Emily. 'And Beethoven does too.'

Beethoven barked in agreement.

'All right,' said Alice. 'We're a lean, mean shopping machine.'

'Great,' said George. 'You don't need my help.'

'No,' Alice said to her husband. 'We'll meet you by the horseshoe pit.'

'Got it,' said George.

Ryce was standing a little apart from the family, looking around her as if expecting – or hoping – to see someone. In fact, all the way up to the lake, Ryce had been daydreaming – daydreaming of seeing Taylor Devereaux. She knew he lived around here someplace, and maybe there was a chance they would run into each other.

'I think I'll walk around a bit,' she said casually. 'You don't have to wait for me. I'll get back to the cottage on my own.'

'Will you be OK?' asked Mr Newton. 'I mean, all by yourself?'

Ryce was already walking away. 'Daddy, in three months I'm going to be driving!'

George turned to Ted. 'Is that true?'

Ted nodded. 'Yup. You want to know how many months until I can drive?'

'No.'

'Fifty-two and a half,' said Ted. 'But it'll go by in the blink of an eye.'

'I'll try not to blink,' said George Newton. 'Listen, we need to build a pen for these little furniture eaters.' He pointed at the puppies who were playing with each other, writhing in the dust on Main Street. 'You mind staying with them while I go into the hardware store?'

Ted took the leashes. 'I'll guard them with my life,' he said.

'Let's hope that won't be necessary.' There was an old man sitting in a chair outside the general store, an old dog at his feet. George nodded to them both.

'Beautiful weather, isn't it?'

'For now,' said the old man.

George knew that old-timers in these little towns usually took some time to warm up to outsiders, so he did his best to be extra friendly. He leaned down to the dog.

'So, does your dog bite?'

'Nope,' said the old man.

Smiling, George put out his hand to pet the old dog. In an instant, the dog snarled and snapped. George pulled his arm back as if he had been stung.

'I thought you said your dog didn't bite!'

'That's not my dog,' said the old man.

Alice and Emily were having a little more luck at the food store. With Beethoven tied to a bicycle rack in front of the shop, mother and daughter made their way inside.

'Now, we're not buying anything silly,' Alice cautioned, 'just basic groceries.'

Emily nodded. She had heard this a hundred times before. 'I know, because we're not millionaires, right?'

'Right.'

'Are we thousandaires?'

Alice pulled open the door of the mini-market and shooed Emily inside. 'Not just yet.'

'Maybe by Christmas?' Emily asked.

Beethoven watched as Alice and Emily went into the shop, then settled down on the warm concrete to wait for their return. But the instant he got comfortable, his sensitive ears picked up a sound. He jumped to his feet and stared down the road. Coming towards him was Regina's red Lexus. Beethoven would have known that car anywhere! Immediately he started barking.

Suddenly Missy appeared in the rear window of the powerful car. She caught sight of Beethoven and her heart jumped with happiness. She barked frantically. Regina immediately smacked her hard.

'Shut up, dumb dog!'

The car raced by and Beethoven tried to follow it. He was tethered to the iron bicycle rack, but he used all his strength to drag it, hauling the pile of metal down the pavement until it got caught between a lamppost and a traffic sign. Grappling with the leather leash, Beethoven barked loudly as the car tore down the road.

Roused by all the commotion, Alice and Emily came racing out of the food store and were surprised to see their beloved pet half-way up the street barking his head off.

Emily immediately fell to her knees next to Beethoven and cradled his big head in her arms.

'What is it, Beethoven? What's wrong?'

Looking up with big sad eyes, Beethoven whined and whimpered. He wished he could tell her . . .

But the little girl understood. 'Mom, Beethoven saw someone,' she said. 'He saw some-one he loves . . .'

Over by the horseshoe pit, Ted was having an

adventure of his own. He was holding the leashes of all four puppies and was staring transfixed as he watched the most beautiful girl he had ever seen in his entire life pitch horseshoes at the metal stake. She was tall and graceful, and she certainly knew how to play the game. She picked up one of the iron rings, and with perfect form launched it at the pole. It wrapped itself around the pole with a clang.

'Good throw, Janie!' said one of the men watching from the town hall steps.

'That's the game,' said another one.

Janie! thought Ted. Her name is Janie. It was the most beautiful name he had ever heard. Then he realized that she was looking right at him and smiling. *Then* he realized that she was heading his way!

'Those are cute puppies,' said Janie. 'Can I pet them?'

'Uh . . . sure,' said Ted.

Bending down, Janie started to caress the little dogs. 'What are their names?'

'Well,' said Ted, 'that one is Chubby and the one next to him is Tchaikovsky. Dolly and Moe. And I'm Ted.'

'Hi there,' said Janie, although Ted couldn't be sure if she was greeting him, the puppies or all of them.

Ted knew he had to act fast. He gathered up all his courage and took a deep breath. 'So – can I buy you a Coke?' As soon as he spoke, he wondered if he had enough money to buy her a Coke. He sure hoped he did.

Janie stood up, raising herself to her full height. She was at least a foot taller than him, and she looked down at him sceptically.

'Aren't I little tall for you?' she asked.

Ted shook his head. 'Not for me. Doesn't bother me one little bit.' Of course, he was wondering just what she meant. Besides, he had offered her a soft drink, not an engagement ring.

'I mean,' Janie persisted, 'don't you think you're a little short?'

Ted shrugged. 'Well, height is just temporary,' he said. 'I mean, you wake up every morning and you're a little taller, right? It happens every day, doesn't it? Things have a way of changing very, very quickly.'

'Well,' said Janie, 'the truth of it is, I wake up taller. *You* probably wake up shorter.' She started to walk away. 'Bye.'

Ted watched her depart, feeling as if his heart had been crushed. He had finally met the girl of his dreams and she was hung up on height. What could he possibly do about that?

Chapter 18

Ryce was walking by the shore of the lake, looking dreamily out over the still, blue water. Suddenly, out of nowhere, she heard the sound of a dirt bike racing down the bank, and a moment later the machine pulled up next to her.

The boy riding it looked like he was about sixteen years old. He wore torn jeans and a T-shirt emblazoned with the name of a heavy metal band that Ryce had never heard of. He had long brown hair that fell to his shoulders.

He was cute and had a nice smile. 'Hi,' he said as he killed the engine of the dirt bike. 'You're new in town, aren't you?'

Ryce nodded. 'That right.'

'What's your name?'

'Ryce,' said Ryce.

'Rice? Like the food?'

Ryce nodded. 'Sort of.'

The boy nodded. 'OK, that's cool. I'm Seth. It's not a food group or anything, but it works. Y'know . . . "Seth, get up. Seth, fix the boat. Seth, you're grounded." It's fairly basic, you know?'

In spite of herself, Ryce smiled. 'Uh-huh.'

'Can I give you a lift somewhere? I've got an extra helmet here.'

Ryce shook her head. 'I'd better not.'

Seth shrugged. 'OK.' He tried to kick the bike back into life. 'Enjoy your summer.'

But the bike wouldn't start. Seth smiled ruefully. 'That's the last time I buy a motorcycle from my father.' Then the engine squealed into life and Seth turned it to go.

'Hey,' Ryce shouted suddenly, 'wait a minute!'

Seth shut down the bike again. 'Changed your mind?'

'Do you know if the Devereaux have a cottage around here? Taylor Devereaux?' She couldn't believe that she was saying his name out loud – and to a complete stranger at that!

Seth gave her a little smile. 'The Devereaux place? Yeah. It's on the west shore. My dad and I haul firewood over there.'

'Can you show me?'

This time the dirt bike came to life instantly. 'Sure. Climb on.'

Ryce pulled on the helmet and climbed on the wide seat behind Seth. They flew down the beach, Seth taking the bumps and hills of the lakeshore like a pro. It didn't take them long to travel the few miles to the house, which sat right on the lake.

Ryce had to admit that she was pretty impressed. The 'cottage' wasn't a cottage at all, but an old lakefront estate that looked as if it dated from the 1920s. There was a big house up on the bluff, with a series of perfect lawns sloping down to the water. At the lake's edge were a long dock and an elaborate gazebo.

Laughter was coming from the gazebo, and suddenly a beautiful blonde girl in a bikini ran out laughing and giggling. A moment later, Taylor followed, chasing the girl down the dock. He caught up with her and tossed her into the water. Her happy screams seemed to fill the air.

Seth wasn't watching Taylor and his antics. His eyes were on Ryce. It was plain to him what was going on – Ryce was very disappointed to find that Taylor had company . . .

'You going to say hello?' he asked.

Ryce didn't take her eyes off Taylor, but she was wise enough to know that she wouldn't be welcome.

'Seth,' she said quietly, 'would you mind taking me home?'

Chapter 19

Alice was putting away the groceries back at the cottage when Emily came into the kitchen with Beethoven trailing behind her.

'Is Daddy still setting up the pen?' Alice asked.

Emily shook her head. 'Nope. He finished it.'

'So what's he doing now?'

'He just told me that he wanted to chop some wood for the fireplace.'

Alice crossed to the kitchen window and peered outside. 'Chop wood? But it's summertime.'

But there was her husband, carefully laying a piece of firewood on the old stump that was used as the surface for splitting logs. He was in the country, and to George Newton the country meant chopping wood.

The four puppies in the makeshift pen sat in a row and watched as George raised his heavy axe. Smiling to himself, George brought the blade down as hard as he could. But he hit the wood off-centre, and the chunk flew up in the air and came down, bouncing off the bumper of George's car.

'Darn it!'

But he refused to be beaten. George took another hunk of wood from the woodpile, placed it on the stump and once again raised his axe – but then he heard a noise at the top of the driveway. It sounded suspiciously like a dirt bike . . .

A second later, Seth and Ryce pulled up. Seth turned off the engine, and Ryce slipped off the machine, pulling at the helmet strap. Seeing his teenage daughter on a motorcycle with a boy with shoulder-length hair, George looked very concerned.

'Hi there,' said Seth amicably.

'Daddy,' said Ryce, 'this is Seth. He gave me a lift from town. Seth, this is my dad.'

'Hello,' said George.

'Nice to meet you,' said Seth. 'Splitting wood?'

George nodded. 'I'm trying.'

Seth plucked a blade of grass and sucked on it. 'Well, don't let us slow you down.'

Determined to show that he knew how to do something as simple as splitting logs, George took a deep breath and let fly with the axe. He struck the piece of wood a glancing blow and sent it flying. Seth almost had to throw himself flat on the ground to avoid being hit by the block of wood! Ryce started to laugh, but stopped when her father glared at her.

But Seth was sympathetic. 'Yeah,' he said knowingly. 'That dogwood is tough stuff.'

George put yet another log on the stump. 'I take it you've chopped some wood in your day.'

Seth nodded. 'Till I was twelve.'

'Why did you stop?' Mr Newton asked, raising the axe high above his head.

'Got a chain-saw,' said Seth.

This piece of good sense put George off his aim completely. The axe fell, missing the log completely, and the blade buried itself up to the handle in the stump.

Seth nodded. 'For me, working with an axe pretty much came down to two things . . .'

Mr Newton was straining to get the axe head out of the wood, but he paused long enough to look over at this curiously self-assured teenager. 'Oh, it did, huh?'

Seth nodded again. 'That's right. First,' he explained, 'you take a look at the log and decide exactly where you want to put your axe.'

George was curious. 'And then?'

'You put it there,' said Seth with a little smile. Then he put all his weight on the kick-start of the dirt bike and the engine burst into life. 'Well,' he shouted, 'it was nice meeting you both.' He spun the machine around and charged up the driveway and out on to the main road.

George watched the boy drive off, then turned an inquiring eye on his daughter. 'You like that guy?'

'I don't know. What do you think of him?'

The question made George feel uncomfortable. He didn't meet Ryce's look. Instead, he busied himself with pulling the axe head from the stump. This was the first conversation on the subject of boys that they had ever had. Mr Newton had a feeling it would not be their last.

'I . . . I think you could do better,' he said finally.

A little smile passed across Ryce's face, as if the thought of her father being uncomfortable amused her. 'OK. If he asks me to marry him, I'll tell him I need some time to think about it. How's that?' Ryce started up towards the house.

'All the same, I don't think you should, y'know –' George shrugged. 'Don't spend a lot of time with him.'

'Daddy – we're only here for the weekend. I probably won't have the chance to see him again.'

'That wouldn't be such a bad thing,' said George under his breath. However, despite how he felt about Seth, he did use the boy's technique for splitting wood. He looked at the log on the stump, saw where he wanted the axe blade to go and with one quick swing cut the log in two clean pieces. George was impressed with what he had done. 'Not bad. Not bad at all.'

Seth? Taylor Devereaux? Ryce was confused, and she decided that she needed to have a talk with her mother. Alice was still in the kitchen.

'Mom, can I ask you a question – I mean, just as a woman, not as a mom?'

'Sure,' said Alice.

Ryce paused a moment. 'When you met Daddy, did you feel something special?'

Alice Newton nodded. 'Yeah.'

'I mean . . . physically.'

'Yeah.'

'Do you still feel it?'

But before Alice could answer, George came sweeping into the kitchen. He had split half a cord of wood and was feeling pretty proud of himself. He was singing at the top of his lungs, and he scooped up his wife and danced her around the kitchen.

'George!' Alice exclaimed, laughing.

He waltzed Alice back to the sink and then skipped happily out of the room, still singing.

'I'm sorry, dear,' said Alice, 'what was the question?'

'Do you *still* feel that way?'

George could be heard bellowing and whooping in another part of the house. 'I think so,' Alice said with a little smile.

Emily was the next to claim her father's attentions. As he came dancing into the living-room, his little daughter jumped up at him, Tchaikovsky clutched in her arms.

'Daddy, can I show you what I've trained Tchaikovsky to do?'

George stopped singing. 'Sure, sweetheart.'

Emily put the puppy down on the floor. 'OK, watch . . . Tchaikovsky – sit!'

The little dog looked up at the little girl and then rolled on the floor, playing with an old shoe he had found somewhere. He didn't want to sit and he didn't care who knew it.

'Well,' said George Newton. 'He was thinking about it. I could tell. Maybe with a little more practice you'll have them all trained.'

'No, no,' insisted Emily. 'He really can do it. Tchaikovsky – sit!'

This time the puppy ignored her completely, not even bothering to look at her.

'I think he's tired of listening to me,' Emily said.

'That is excellent preparation for having children of your own,' said Mr Newton.

But Emily had more tricks up her sleeve. She picked up a small stick she had brought in from outside and held it under the puppy's wet little nose.

'Tchaikovsky – fetch!' With all her might, she threw the stick to the far side of the room. The little dog made no attempt to go after the stick.

Instead, Tchaikovsky looked at her, a puzzled expression on his face, then, without warning, sat down on his fat little rump! He looked very pleased with himself.

'You know,' said Emily. 'I don't think he speaks too much English yet.'

Chapter 20

Later that night, after Emily had gone to bed and Ted was snug in his room reading, Ryce decided that she would take a walk by the lake. It wasn't that late and it was still quite light out, so George and Alice let her go – on the condition that she took Beethoven with her.

Beethoven could sense that Ryce had something on her mind, so he walked along ahead of her at the very end of his leash, giving her plenty of room.

In spite of herself, Ryce knew that there was only one way she wanted to go, and she made no attempt to prevent herself from walking down the beach towards Taylor Devereaux's house. Maybe he was alone now and maybe they could just sit on the dock and talk about things, get to know each other a little better.

But things didn't quite turn out the way she had hoped. As she got nearer and nearer to the Devereaux house, she could hear loud, raucous music playing and the occasional shout. She didn't have to get too close to realize that there was a big party in progress at the Devereauxs' place.

Ryce peered at the house and could make out a

number of people on the dock and on the porch at the front of the house. Even from far away, Ryce could see that the kids at the house were older than she was, closer to Taylor's age than her own.

Beethoven watched the house too, and he didn't like what he saw. The fur stood up on the back of his neck and he barked at Ryce, as if warning her about something.

'What?' she asked. 'What's the matter?'

Beethoven looked up at her questioningly, then, turning, he started pulling her back the way they had come. Laughing, Ryce held on to the leash and allowed herself to be hauled down the beach.

'OK, OK. Whatever you say!' Suddenly, Taylor Devereaux didn't seem quite so important to her. She didn't know if it was because she had met Seth or if it was just that she was coming to her senses.

Suddenly, a bright light shone in her eyes and she was blinded for a moment. Someone was standing on the lawn of the house shining a flashlight in her face.

'Ryce?'

But Ryce could only squint into the bright white light.

'It's me – Taylor.' The light snapped out and

Taylor ran over, dropping down to the beach from the lawn. Taylor looked genuinely glad to see her – but Beethoven wasn't glad to see him! He growled softly at the boy, as if warning him to keep his distance from Ryce.

But Taylor paid no attention to the dog. He smiled at Ryce, flashing his blue eyes at her. In spite of herself, Ryce felt her heart melt a little.

'This is so far out!' exclaimed Taylor. 'Where did you come from?'

'We . . . we were taking a walk,' she stammered. 'I . . . I guess I didn't know you lived around here.' Ryce hated lying, but she couldn't bring herself to admit to him that she had been wandering around in the dark hoping to get a glimpse of him.

'Yeah,' said Taylor, 'this is the cottage. Only my parents are away so we're doing the party thing. Come on up, I'll show you around.'

Ryce wanted to stay, but something inside her told her she shouldn't. 'I don't know . . .' she said uncertainly.

Stepping behind her, Taylor started to push her up the beach towards the house. 'Come on,' he said playfully, 'at least come and see the view. Wow, you're heavy!' She felt his hands snake down to her ribs, and he began tickling her. Ryce giggled – Beethoven growled.

'OK!' said Ryce. 'OK!'

Taylor glanced down at Beethoven. 'Maybe you'd better tie up your dog. My parents have a lot of carpets and stuff. We wouldn't want him to do any damage, would we?'

'OK,' said Ryce. She wrapped Beethoven's chain around one of the posts supporting the deck and followed Taylor up the steps to the house.

There were lots of boys and girls jammed on to the deck and in the living-room, and the music was blaring from a dozen speakers scattered here and there. All of the kids were older than Ryce – not only that, they seemed to be older than Taylor himself. This was a college age group, and they were sprawled everywhere, drinking beer. Cigarette smoke hung in the air.

Taylor took Ryce's hand and led her through the crowd.

'The drinks are over here,' he shouted over the music, leading her to a bar overflowing with bottles. There were a couple of college guys standing around the drinks, and they leered at Ryce. They were a little drunk, and that made Ryce nervous.

Taylor pulled a can of beer from the cooler. 'You want a beer?'

Ryce shook her head. 'No, just a glass of water, please.'

'Hey,' said one of the guys, 'why don't you stretch a little? Embrace the spirit.'

'I don't drink,' said Ryce. The situation was making her feel uncomfortable, and she looked to Taylor for help.

But the older kid would not be dissuaded. He thrust a cold can of beer into her hand. 'How do you know you don't drink? Maybe you *do* drink but you just don't know about it yet.' He and the rest of his cronies brayed with laughter.

Taylor took charge. 'Look, Howard,' he said firmly, 'if she doesn't want to drink, she doesn't want to drink.'

'Affirmative. My sincere apologies,' said Howard. The college kids backed off immediately, and Ryce was so grateful to Taylor she could have kissed him.

But if Ryce wasn't going to drink, it certainly wasn't going to stop Howard and his pals. He held up his can of beer and waved it at his companions. 'Gentlemen, what time is it?'

They answered in a chorus, 'It's brewski time!' Then they all chugged down their beers. Watching from below on the beach, Beethoven growled and pulled his chain as tight as it would go, straining to keep Ryce in sight.

Ryce felt awkward and ill at ease, and she

started edging away from the crowd. 'I think maybe I should go now . . .'

Taylor was soothing and sincere. 'Please,' he said, 'just come and see the view from upstairs. It's the best thing in the house.'

Against her better judgement, Ryce allowed herself to be pulled towards the stairs. 'OK,' she said, 'but right after that I'm going.'

Taylor nodded. 'Absolutely.'

At the top of the stairs, Taylor opened a door and lead Ryce into a room. It was an elegantly furnished bedroom.

'You know,' said Taylor softly, 'this is really strange – I had a dream about you just the other day. Has that ever happened to you? Strange, huh? You dream about someone and then you run into them?'

'Uh . . . not exactly.' Ryce's eyes were drawn to the far side of the room – a wall of tall windows looked out over the lake. She could see the dark blue of the water, the blue-black of the star-dappled night sky, a full yellow moon hanging just above the horizon. Ryce had to admit, the view *was* beautiful.

'Wow,' she said, gazing out at the still water.

Behind her, Taylor smiled and, as quietly as possible, locked the door. But Ryce heard the click as the mechanism slipped into place, and she turned quickly.

'Did you just lock the door?' she asked, alarmed.

Taylor waved the key on a chain. 'Don't worry. The key is right here . . .' He came up and stood next to her. 'I just wanted to make sure that we had some privacy.'

Ryce tried to control the panic that was rising in her. 'No – unlock it. Right now!'

But Taylor ignored her. Instead, he draped an arm across her shoulder and turned her face to his. 'Remember when we kissed in my car? I still think about that.'

From the beach, Beethoven could see Ryce at the window and he whimpered and stirred uneasily. His cries turned to a deep growl when he saw Taylor move in close to her. Then he barked loudly.

'Hey, look!' Howard shouted. 'A dog!' Howard and his friends peered down from the deck. 'Hey, big guy! You want a beer?'

Beethoven growled and barked again.

'He said yes,' said one of Howard's cronies.

'Yeah, right,' said Howard, 'like you speak dog.'

'Of course I do,' his friend responded. 'My girlfriend is a dog!' He was so drunk he thought this was uproariously funny. Screaming with laughter, he pulled out a fresh beer and pulled the tab.

'Yo!' he yelled. 'What time is it?'

All the guys at the railing yelled as loud as they could: 'It's brewski time!'

'No – it's brewski time for Fido!'

They all popped open the cans and poured them over the side of the balcony, splashing Beethoven with beer. Beethoven ducked and pulled away hard, trying to avoid the falling liquid.

'Operation Brewski for Fido!'

'Operation Wide Poochie,' yelled Howard. 'Beer storm moving in!'

Beethoven strained at his leash. He was getting very angry . . .

On the second floor of the house, Taylor was unaware of the storm that was brewing down on the deck. He was more interested in romancing Ryce. He sat down on the bed and patted the place next to him.

'C'mon – sit down on the bed and talk to me.'

Ryce was in no mood to play. 'Unlock the door,' she said seriously.

Taylor smiled his most charming smile. 'Look, there's nothing to worry about. I'll hang the key right here on the bedpost. Now, come sit down and talk to me.'

'No,' said Ryce. 'Open the door. Now!'

Downstairs, more beer spattered around Beethoven and he barked angrily.

'Hey!' shouted Howard. 'I think we're annoying the little doggy! Whatsamatta, poochie? Want some more?' He tossed a full beer can right at Beethoven – and that was enough!

Snarling, Beethoven leapt forward, yanking his chain taut. And that was all it took to yank the deck off its supports. Suddenly it tilted at a steep angle, pitching all of the drunk college boys into the water!

The support for the deck also held up the roof. Now the only thing holding it together was two old rusty chains which ran at an angle up to the second storey. The instant the deck collapsed, the second storey wall started to peel away. The whole front of the house was coming apart!

'You don't seem to understand,' said Taylor. 'You and I are going to have an experience you'll never forget.'

Ryce was really scared now. 'No. Let me out of here.'

'Magic,' said Taylor. 'C'mon, look at the view. The moon. There's only one thing missing.' He leaned against the wall, but before his arm actually touched it the entire wall of the bedroom collapsed in a shower of plaster and Taylor fell right through the hole!

There was a scream and then a bump. Then a big splash as Taylor tumbled straight into the lake!

Quickly, Ryce unlocked the door and ran downstairs to look at the damage. Most of the house was in the water, and all the party guests were thrashing around in the lake. Beethoven was sitting on the beach, watching all the trouble he had caused. He looked pretty pleased with himself. He barked happily when he saw Ryce.

'Good dog!' said Ryce. She bent down and gave her faithful dog a big hug. 'I think we'd better go home now.' Together they raced off into the darkness.

The party-goers stumbled out of the water. Taylor was in shock – his parents were going to kill him! But Howard and the rest of the guys were delighted.

Howard clapped Taylor on the back. 'Taylor, man, great party!'

Chapter 21

One of the best things about Lake MacDonald was the traditional country fair the village put on every Fourth of July. The whole Newton family looked forward to walking into town to see the crafts and the exhibits. There was even a little carnival featuring a small Ferris wheel, a merry-go-round and some games of chance.

As far as George Newton was concerned, the best part about the fairs was the delicious food, particularly the juicy hamburgers and French fries.

'I'm hungry,' said George. 'Is anybody else hungry?' Beethoven looked up happily. Did someone mention food? It was one of his favourite subjects.

'Let's look around a little first,' said Alice.

'I want to go on the rides,' said Emily. 'Can I go and get tickets? I have my own money.'

'OK,' said Alice. 'Ted, will you go with her?'

'Sure.'

'And stay together,' said George.

'Come on, Beethoven,' said Emily. The two kids and their dog ran off to join the queue for tickets.

Looking up to the front of the queue, Ted saw Janie and his heart did a little flip. She was just getting her strip of tickets when a bigger kid grabbed them out of her hand.

Janie tried to snatch them back, but he held them above her head, taunting her. Some of his cronies laughed.

'Give them back, goof!' shouted Janie.

'What's the matter, Janie? In a bad mood today? Don'tcha wanna have a little fun?'

Ted felt his blood burning in his veins. No one was going to get away with that kind of thing – not while he was around.

'C'mon, Beethoven,' he said. The boy and the dog raced over to the crowd of boys who were tormenting Janie. Ted stopped in front of them and put on his absolutely dorkiest face.

'Hey,' he squeaked, 'want to see what I taught my dog?'

All of the bigger boys stared at him. 'Who's this runt?'

'No, watch . . .' said Ted. 'Beethoven, sit!'

Beethoven immediately did as he was told.

'Beat it, dorkmeister,' said one of the kids.

Ted just grinned. 'Wait! Just one more. Beethoven, bark!'

Beethoven barked!

'Hey, I said beat it, small fry.'

'OK,' said Ted. 'This is the last one. I promise. Beethoven, when I give the signal, bite this guy on the wiener.'

Looking up at the boys, Beethoven growled and snarled, baring his big white teeth. His jaws snapped as if he couldn't *wait* to do what Ted commanded.

Suddenly, the big kids weren't laughing any more. Beethoven looked as if he would be *very* disappointed if he didn't get a chance to chomp them all into little pieces. Janie beamed at Ted.

'Beat it, dorkmeister,' Ted ordered, grabbing the tickets from the kid's hand. Beethoven kept his eyes locked on the boys until they were safely far away.

Janie looked very grateful. 'Thanks,' she said. 'You're Ed, right?'

'Ted,' said Ted.

'Can I buy you a Coke, Ted?'

Ted played it cool. 'I'd love to, but I have to take a rain-check.' He nodded towards Emily, who was still standing in line waiting to buy her tickets. 'I've got responsibilities.'

'Maybe later?' asked Janie hopefully.

'Yeah . . . Later.' Ted strolled back to the queue, feeling very pleased with himself – and delighted with his dog.

'Did you really teach Beethoven to bite someone in the wiener?' Emily asked.

Ted shook his head. 'No. But he knew what I meant.' He ruffled the fur on the back of Beethoven's neck. 'Didn't you, boy?'

Beethoven just smiled!

Ryce was browsing in the craft section of the fair, admiring a quilt, when she felt someone tap her on the shoulder. She turned. It was Seth – and she was surprised how happy she felt to see him.

'Hi,' said Ryce.

'How's it going?'

'Pretty good,' said Ryce.

'You here with your family?'

'Yeah,' said Ryce squirming in embarrassment. 'You know how it is . . .'

But Seth didn't care. 'Listen,' he said earnestly, 'I have to work at the marina till five. But afterwards, do you want to go on a picnic or something? We could go for a walk, talk, whatever?'

Unlike Taylor Devereaux, she knew she could trust Seth. But she couldn't see him . . .

Ryce's smile faded slightly. 'Well, actually, I can't . . . My dad kind of told me not to see you.'

Seth looked confused and a little hurt. 'Why? Why would he tell you that?'

Ryce shrugged. This was really hard to deal with. 'I don't know. 'Cause he's a dad, I guess.'

Seth's face fell and he blushed slightly. 'Well . . . I guess I'd better get going.' He retreated a few steps, then stopped and turned. 'Enjoy the rest of your summer, Ryce.'

'You too.' Ryce hated herself for hurting his feelings, but she didn't know what else to do. Growing up was more difficult than she had ever imagined it would be.

Chapter 22

Ted, Emily and Beethoven strolled through the fairgrounds looking at all the stands. There was a collection of flowers and vegetables grown by gardeners in the Lake MacDonald area – huge watermelons and squashes, as well as beautiful roses and tulips with blooms as big as coffee cups. There were also contest stands – cutest baby, tallest man, ugliest cat – and one in particular absolutely fascinated Beethoven.

Sitting at a long table on a portable stage was a collection of big men and even bigger dogs – a sheepdog, a German Shepherd and a Great Dane.

'Now there's a hungry-looking dog,' one of the men said to Ted. He pointed at Beethoven. 'You going to sign him up?'

'Sign him up for what?' asked Ted.

The man pointed to a sign: Pet & Owner Burger Binge. 1st Prize – 500 lbs of dog food.

'What's a burger binge?' asked Emily.

'It's an eating contest,' the man explained. 'For pets and their owners.'

Ted turned to his sister. 'What do you think?'

'Beethoven and Daddy, you mean?'

'That's exactly what I mean!'

George Newton was very reluctant to enter the contest, but the whole family pulled him towards the special events tent.

'Oh, I don't know . . .'

'Come on,' said Alice. 'It'll be fun.'

'Me making a fool of myself will be fun?'

'Yes,' said Alice and Ryce simultaneously.

'You said you were hungry,' said Emily.

Just then, the public address system crackled into life. 'All contestants for the burger binge, please report to the special events tent!'

'That's you, Daddy!' said Emily.

'Please . . .' pleaded George.

'It'll be something for the kids to tell their children, George.'

'OK, OK . . .'

The competition looked pretty fierce. All of the contestants were seated at the table with their dogs next to them. One of the judges stepped on to the stage and spoke into his microphone.

'Ladies and gentlemen, welcome to our seventh annual burger binge. In position number one, the team of Barry Mondello and Ringo!'

The audience cheered as a big fat man stood up, holding the paw of a hairy sheepdog.

'In position two, Sergeant Arthur Lewis and

Wolfgang!' A burly Marine waved to the crowd and raised the paw of his dog, a big German Shepherd.

'And contestant number three, last year's champions – Tree MacKinnon and Jaws!'

The applause was loudest for Tree, who proudly stood and raised the paw of an enormous Great Dane. The dog jumped up on its hind legs – and he seemed to be just as tall as his owner.

'Hungry, Tree?' asked the judge.

'Starving!' shouted Tree MacKinnon.

'Attaboy! And last but not least – George Newton and Beethoven.'

Alice and the kids applauded as loudly as possible.

'OK,' said the judge, 'bring on the burgers!'

As the audience applauded, a line of women walked out from behind the curtain and made their way to the stage. Each one carried a big bowl of burgers that they placed in front of the contestants. As George and Beethoven looked on, Tree had to hold his Great Dane by the collar to keep the dog from starting to eat before the starter gave the word.

The judge held up his hands, calling for quiet. 'There are the same number of burgers in each bowl. The first team to finish wins. Any questions?'

George raised his hand. 'Yes. Are there knives and forks?'

The judge shook his head. ''Fraid not, George. Just hands and paws. Contestants – are you ready?'

Mr Newton carefully spread his napkin in his lap and nodded that he was ready.

'Get set!'

'This is barbaric,' George whispered to Beethoven. 'Absolutely barbaric.'

'Go!' said the judge.

Side by side, the contestants and their dogs started wolfing down the burgers. Crowding to the front of the stage, the excited audience cheered on their favourites. But as George took his first bite, he noticed that Beethoven was just sitting there.

'What are you waiting for? Eat!'

With a happy bark, Beethoven dived into the bowl of food, eating as if he had been starved for a month.

Suddenly, every person in the competition was eating burgers as though they were piranha fish. Alice and the kids chanted, 'Go, George! Go, George! Go!' And he did his best – but he couldn't keep up with Beethoven. He was sucking up burg like a vacuum cleaner!

It became obvious that Tree MacKinnon and

Jaws were the team to beat. Man and beast were eating like creatures possessed – as if they hadn't eaten in weeks and there was a good chance they wouldn't eat again for six months!

George looked at Tree and his dog, and he began to think that there was no way he could beat them. His spirits flagging, he took smaller and smaller bites. But Alice wouldn't let him lose. She jumped on to the stage and yelled at her husband.

'George, remember when you were little and your dad was out of work? Remember how hungry you'd get? Eat, George, eat!'

George remembered those unhappy childhood days well. He took a big bite from his burger and chewed quickly. He was picking up momentum again. He finished one burger and grabbed for another and stuffed it in his mouth.

But Tree and Jaws were still ahead. 'This is for the kids, George,' said Alice. 'They're going to remember this. They don't know about air fresheners, George. *This* is what they're going to remember!'

A fiery look lit George's eyes. Ask him to do something for his children and there was no stopping him.

'Show them what their dad is made of!' Alice urged. 'Show them!'

Straightening up, George started eating with both hands, chomping through burgers in a single bite. Seeing George suddenly get a second wind like that, Tree MacKinnon started to slow down, looking a little nervous.

'Daddy! Daddy! Daddy!' the Newton kids chanted as they jumped up and down.

Beethoven did his part to win the contest, gulping down burgers as if he were a big, hairy hamburger-eating machine.

George and Tree were neck and neck now. Each reached for a burger and then stopped to take a breath and to take a look at the other's progress. Each of them had one burger left in the bowl, and you could tell by the look on each man's face that the last one was going to be torture.

Tree stuffed the second to last burger into his face and swallowed it. George tried to follow suit but he seemed to slow down, his cheeks bulging out. With difficulty, he fought down the burger and then reached for the last – but it was gone!

Beethoven had snatched it out of the bowl and swallowed it in the winking of an eye. George grabbed the bowl and held it upside down, proving that it was empty.

The judge blew his whistle. 'We have a winner!'

The crowd cheered and the whole Newton family, including the puppies, ran on to the stage to hug George. Sitting side by side, George and Beethoven looked at each other, then belched in unison.

Chapter 23

Winning the burger-eating contest made the Newton family (and their dogs) celebrities at the fair, and it wasn't long before a middle-aged couple walked up to them and started petting the dogs.

'Just look at those puppies,' said the woman. 'Friskier than anything!'

'Happy Independence Day, folks,' said the woman's husband. He took George's hand and pumped it. 'I'm Cliff Klamath. How you all doin'?'

'I'm George Newton. And I guess we're doing pretty good. A little full, but . . .'

Cliff joined his wife in petting the pups. They all started barking, except for Tchaikovsky, who buried his needle-sharp teeth in the cloth of Cliff's trouser leg.

Mr Newton tried to dislodge the puppy. 'Tchaikovsky! Stop that! I'm awfully sorry,' he said to Cliff. 'Sometimes they forget their manners.'

But Cliff didn't seem to mind. He just laughed heartily. 'Don't I know it,' he said affably. 'I'm in the business myself.'

'The business?' asked Alice.

Cliff just laughed again. 'The dog business. You need 'em, we breed 'em. Our place is just half-way up the mountain.' Still smiling, he handed over his business card.

George read it out for the whole family. 'Triple A Breeding Kennels. Cliff and Mona Klamath, proprietors.'

'How do you do,' said Mona.

'Anyway,' said Cliff, 'I don't want to take up too much of your time. If you haven't got plans for these pups, we might be interested in taking them off your hands.'

'Really?' said George.

'Sure. For a purebred litter like this, we pay a pretty fair buck.'

Making a fair buck was something near and dear to Mr Newton's heart, but he knew he could never sell the puppies. Not now . . .

'I don't think so,' he said, shaking his head. 'They're sort of family.'

'That's a pity,' said Cliff, looping his thumbs into his braces. 'I wouldn't be surprised if Mona here – she's the banker, you know – I wouldn't be surprised if she dug deep into her pockets for those little St Bernards . . .'

'No,' said Alice, 'we couldn't possibly –'

Cliff raised his voice a little, cutting her off.

'Now, before you say no, consider this. Mona, what kind of figure are we talking about here? Just to show Mr Newton that we ain't trying to cheat him.'

Mona scratched her head. 'Well, giving it some thought, I sincerely feel that these puppies are worth four hundred dollars each!'

'Four hundred dollars?' said George Newton. That was a *lot* of money.

'That's sixteen hundred dollars cash,' said Mona. 'For puppies you don't really need.'

'Sixteen hundred dollars for four puppies,' her husband added. 'Lemme tell you, you're not gonna do any better than that.'

George was tempted. Money was very tight – tight at work, tight at home – and an extra one thousand six hundred would certainly come in handy . . .

But before he could say a word, a strident female voice yelled behind him.

'Excuse me. But those puppies are mine!'

Everyone turned. It was Regina!

The instant Beethoven saw her, he leapt forward, snarling and snapping. George had hold of the leash and he pulled back hard. 'Beethoven! No!'

Regina did a little snarling of her own. 'Keep that mutt away from me!'

'Did I hear you say these puppies are yours?' asked Cliff Klamath.

'That's right! They were born to my St Bernard, in my apartment building, under my supervision. These children stole them from me.' She jabbed a finger at Ted and Emily. 'If they're worth anything, the money belongs to me!'

Alice Newton was flabbergasted. 'I beg your pardon?'

Regina bent over Ted and Emily. The boy and the girl shrunk away in terror. 'You weren't selling candy bars in my building! You were dog-napping!'

'Mommy,' said Emily. 'I'm scared!'

'What is going on?' demanded George Newton.

'Your children are thieves,' said Regina calmly. 'They lied about why they were in my building, and they took my puppies without permission '

'Now, just hold on a minute,' said George.

'*You* hold on, mister!' snapped Regina. 'You're very lucky I haven't charged them with grand theft.'

Alice couldn't believe her ears, but this woman – no matter how unpleasant – did seem genuinely angry. Alice turned to Ted and Emily. 'Is this true?'

'Yes,' said Ted slowly. 'But they were Beethoven's puppies too!'

George was amazed. 'You mean, you knew they were hers and you took them?'

'But she was going to drown them,' Emily wailed.

Regina snorted. 'Drown puppies worth sixteen hundred dollars? I hardly think so. Now, hand them over.'

Ted and Emily looked close to tears. Ryce was upset too. 'Do we have to, Daddy?'

George nodded. 'If she owns the mother . . . I guess the puppies are hers.'

Big fat tears rolled down Emily's cheeks. 'But she was going to drown them! I *heard* her!'

'Are you going to hand them over – or do I have to call the police?' yelled Regina.

Alice was grim-faced. 'You'd better give them back,' she said quietly.

As Ted handed the four leashes to Regina, Emily hid her face against Alice's leg and sobbed bitterly, as if her heart would break.

Mr Newton turned to Regina. 'I promise you, they will never do anything like this again.'

Regina smiled nastily. 'Well, if they do, I'll have them arrested.' She yanked the puppies and started to walk away, then she stopped and smiled coyly at the Klamaths.

'Any idea where a business-minded dog owner could get a cup of coffee around here?'

Cliff nodded. 'Yessiree! There's a café right around the corner, and my wife and I would be pleased to show you where it is. Wouldn't we, Mona?'

'We most surely would,' said Mona. The Klamaths didn't care who they bought the puppies from.

As Regina and the breeders started to walk away, Beethoven tried to run after them, pulling so forcefully on his leash that George was almost yanked off his feet. Emily threw her arms around Beethoven's neck, and Ryce and Ted grabbed him by the collar.

'Beethoven! Don't! Please,' begged Ryce.

But Beethoven ignored her. His eyes were fixed on his little puppies as they were pulled along by the evil woman. He let out a long, heartrending howl.

All four of the little puppies turned and looked at their father with droopy sad eyes and barked their little barks before they were yanked around a corner and out of sight.

Emily just couldn't stop crying. 'That lady hated the puppies!' she wailed. 'She just wanted them back so she could sell them!'

Ted was desperately trying to think of a plan. 'We could buy them back. If you lend us the money, we'll get part-time jobs.'

'Yeah,' said Ryce. 'We could get a morning paper round and I could work at McDonald's. It wouldn't take that long to get the money.'

Alice shook her head sadly. 'It's not that simple. We spent what we had on the new machinery, and the bank won't lend us any more. And after the new line comes out it will still be ninety days before we see any money. In the meantime, we've got enough to feed ourselves and go to the movies once in a while. And that's about it.'

'Maybe we could sell the TV,' said Ted eagerly.

'Yeah. The puppies are better than the TV,' put in Emily.

'Please,' said Alice. 'It's over. They're gone and that's it.'

But Alice was as upset as everyone else. Unable to face her children, she turned away. George Newton looked down at his family and then at Beethoven's big sad eyes.

'No . . .' he said, his voice firm. 'I'm going to get them back!'

'You're what?' asked Alice, astonished.

'You wait here,' he said. Everyone watched in amazement as George took off, running in the direction that Regina and the puppies had taken. He trailed them all the way to the coffee shop and got there just in time to see the Klamaths writing a cheque to Regina.

'Wait . . . Please,' he said, out of breath. 'I'll pay the sixteen hundred dollars.'

Regina just sneered at him. 'You?'

The puppies gathered around George's ankles, yipping happily. They were delighted to see him. 'My children love these puppies,' he said, pleading with the woman. 'Please let me buy them.'

'Go away,' said Regina disdainfully.

'It's so important to us,' George begged. 'The Klamaths have lots of dogs. But these are special to us. It's for my kids.'

Regina nodded. 'OK. I'll sell them to you and your brats. The price is two thousand bucks.'

George was taken aback. 'But you were going to get sixteen hundred.'

Regina checked her flawless red fingernails. 'That's right.'

'So,' said Mr Newton, 'why do I have to pay two thousand?'

'Oh,' said Regina, 'I don't know.' She flashed him a cruel smile. 'Just for fun.'

George looked into her mean little eyes and for a moment was going to tell her off, to really let this heartless woman know what he thought of her . . . Then he thought of his tearful family. He took out his cheque-book and slowly began writing.

Chapter 24

That night, when the whole Newton family was sound asleep, Beethoven crept off the sofa and crawled into the tiny laundry room off the kitchen. Climbing into the utility sink, Beethoven jammed his nose under the half-open window, raised it a few inches higher, then crawled out into the night.

As he dashed by the puppies' pen, all four of the little dogs heard their father and immediately started yipping quietly and scratching at the wire, trying to get out and follow him. Chubby managed to squirm under the wire, so Beethoven had to rush back and nudge the little dog back into the pen. He woofed quietly, ordering his unruly children to stay put.

Then he was off, running along the dirt road into the village and across the empty town green where the fair had been held just that afternoon. On the field, Beethoven's sensitive nose picked up Regina's scent, and in a flash he was tracking her down the road.

Beethoven didn't have to go too far out of town before he found the turn-off that marked Regina's driveway. Then he saw the car and the cottage beyond it. Light was pouring from the windows of the house and there was loud music playing, as if there were a celebration going on. Beethoven stood on his hind legs and peered in the window.

Floyd and Regina were dancing around the living-room, drinking champagne. They looked very happy.

'A million bucks!' yelled Floyd. 'And it's almost ours!'

'Mine,' corrected Regina. 'And don't forget the easy two thousand I picked up from that sap George Newton! To think I was gonna drown those cute little beasts.'

'Yeah!' agreed Floyd. 'For that kind of dough maybe you oughta spend your million on a puppy farm.'

Regina looked at her boyfriend with scorn. 'Yeah, right.'

Beethoven was pretty sure that Floyd and Regina would never know he was there. He darted around the house and put all his weight on the door leading down to the basement. Leaving a trail of muddy paw prints, Beethoven stole down the stairs.

In the basement, Missy tried to jump to her feet when Beethoven ran into the room – but the cage was far too small to allow her to move at all! The only thing she could do was whimper and rub her nose against his poking through the bars.

Beethoven had no trouble lifting the latch of the cage with his paws, and in an instant Missy was free. She leapt forward and licked him on the face, nuzzling into her rescuer. Full of joy, Beethoven licked back.

Then Beethoven guided his lady love towards the door, and a second later they were running out into the night – to freedom!

But Missy wasn't the only dog to gain freedom that night. Chubby, Moe, Tchaikovsky and Dolly waited patiently for their father to return, but when he didn't, the puppies began to get anxious. By dawn, they had had enough. Slowly but surely, Chubby worked his way back under the chicken wire. It took a while, but after some hard work, he wormed his way through the fence. A second later, his brothers and sisters followed.

The four sharp noses of the puppies quickly picked up their daddy's scent, and in a second they were scampering down the road after him, running as fast their stubby little legs would allow.

*

Emily was the first to notice that Beethoven and his puppies were missing. She woke up early and, as was her habit, wandered outside to look for Beethoven and the rest of the dogs.

The instant she saw the puppy pen, her sleepy eyes opened wide. 'Uh-oh,' she said. She ran back inside and immediately roused the entire house.

The whole family gathered to inspect the pen.

'You have to admit,' said Ted, 'those puppies are pretty darn smart.'

'They probably haven't gone far,' said George Newton.

Emily crossed her arms. *She* knew exactly what had happened to the puppies. 'They've gone to that lady's house,' she said, 'to look for their mom.'

'Why do you say that?' asked Alice.

'Because they missed their mommy,' said Emily. 'So did Beethoven.'

George looked at Alice. All Alice could do was look back and shrug.

'We should go there and look,' insisted Emily.

'Honey,' said George, 'even if you were right, we don't know where she lives.'

'You know her name, don't you?' said Ted.

Mr Newton nodded. 'Yes, Regina Davidson. But she won't be in the phone book or anything. She's just renting.'

'Someone must know where she lives,' said Alice.

Ryce had a little smile on her face. '*I* know who'd know,' she said.

Ryce knew that *Seth* would know!

He had a little time to spare that morning, so he drove Ryce and Mr Newton up towards Regina's cottage, while Mrs Newton followed with Ted and Emily in the family station wagon. The house was a good way up Copper Mountain.

'This is ridiculous,' grumbled George. 'Those puppies would never have found their way up here!'

'You can never tell with animals,' said Seth. He stepped on the brake and the Jeep lurched to a halt.

'What's the matter?' asked George, alarmed.

Seth tossed his long hair. 'The cottage is about a hundred yards up the road. You want me to take you right in?'

'No,' said George. 'I'll handle it from here. Thank you for your trouble.'

That morning, Regina and Floyd had discovered that *their* dog was missing as well. The two of them stared dumbly at the empty cage and the sets of paw prints on the concrete floor.

'There are dog tracks going in,' said Floyd, 'and dog tracks going out – how did she get so muddy sitting in her cage?'

Regina rolled her eyes. 'They're not her tracks, pinhead. Another dog must have come in and let her out.'

'Pretty strange,' said Floyd. Then his eye caught something moving on the lawn. It was all the puppies – each sniffing in circles on the garden.

'They're looking for something,' said Floyd.

'Their looking for their parents, Einstein . . . And a million bucks says they find 'em. All we have to do is follow them.'

'They're headed up the mountain,' said Floyd.

'Then so are we!'

As Regina and Floyd trekked out of the back garden of the house, following the puppies, George Newton and his family were coming up the driveway.

'The car is here,' said George, 'but the place looks deserted.'

'I'm sure they wouldn't mind if we looked around a little.'

The two adults and the kids fanned out and began searching the area.

'Puppies!' shouted Emily. 'Oh, puppies!'

'You know,' said George uneasily, 'technically this is trespassing. I mean, we have no reason to believe they even came here.'

'Well, if we get in trouble, we can always plead insanity,' said Alice.

Ted was the farthest along, just at the edge of the grass and at the beginning of the trail that led farther up the mountain. Suddenly, he cried out. 'Look! Puppy poop! It's theirs. I'm sure it is.' Ted looked up the trail. 'St Bernards are mountain dogs,' the boy said. 'I bet they went up the mountain.'

'Mountain dogs,' said George. 'They've never seen a mountain in their lives.'

'It doesn't matter,' Ted countered. 'It's in their blood. Come on . . .'

The kids hurried up the trail, with Alice and George lagging behind them.

'What are we doing here?' said Mr Newton.

'That's simple,' said Alice. 'Mister Fun is going on a family adventure.'

George looked up the steep trail and further up at the dark clouds gathering around the peak of Copper Mountain. 'Some adventure!'

Alice urged her husband up the trail, and gradually George got into the spirit of the escapade. Suddenly he stopped and knelt down, staring at a small tree.

'Look!' he said.

Everyone stopped and looked, but they couldn't see anything.

'What?' asked Ryce.

'See where the bark's been chewed off at the bottom of this tree? These tooth marks are too big for a mouse, and a deer or bear would chew further up the trunk. *That*, children, was made by a hungry puppy.'

All three kids looked at their father with great respect. 'Cool,' said Ted.

Emily was thrilled. 'I knew they were here!'

Ryce, Ted and Emily raced up the pathway, while George turned to Alice. 'You know,' he said, 'before I met you, I was quite a Boy Scout.'

'There's no chance that it could have been a squirrel that made those marks?'

George nodded. 'It could have been a squirrel,' he admitted.

Suddenly the low grumble of thunder rolled across the sky. Alice looked up. 'How are you at predicting the weather?'

'I'm good at it,' said George. 'It's going to rain.' Just then a fat raindrop landed in the middle of his head. 'See. Told you.'

Regina and Floyd knew nothing about the woods, and they hadn't gone far before they were aching from twisted ankles and scraped knees.

However, because they had a head start on the Newtons, it was Regina and Floyd who found the puppies first. The pups had been thrown off the scent by the rain, and when the man and woman found them the dogs were wandering around the trail sniffing at the damp ground.

'They've lost the scent,' said Regina.

Lifting his head in despair, Chubby started to bark. The other puppies watched him for a moment, then they joined in, adding their high-pitched little barks.

From further up the trail came an answering bark. Beethoven and Missy were sheltering in a little cave. Their joyful howls echoed down the valley, urging their little children forward to safety.

Hearing their parents barking, the four puppies happily took off up the slope – but with Chubby a few feet behind.

Of course, the puppies weren't the only ones who heard the joyous barks of Missy and Beethoven. Regina smiled as the echoes died away.

'You hear that sound?' she asked Floyd.

Floyd had tumbled into a deep hole at the side of the trail, and he was doing his best to climb out of it. 'Yeah?'

'That's the sound of money,' said Regina, already charging up the trail. 'Will you just get moving?'

Chapter 25

The four puppies scrambled up the trail and into the waiting licks and nuzzles of their happy parents. Missy and Beethoven swept their babies into the cosy little cave and lay down next to them to keep them warm and safe. *Finally*, the puppies and their mom and dad were reunited and happy. It had taken so long, but it had finally happened!

But it wasn't going to last.

The instant the happy little furry family settled in their cave Floyd came bursting in followed closely by Regina. Missy and Beethoven jumped to their feet and growled at the same time, their eyes fixed on their two enemies.

'Get the big one away, Floyd, so I can get the muzzle on Missy,' Regina ordered.

Floyd moved in, poking his big stick into Beethoven's ribs. Beethoven was angry, and he snapped viciously at the man.

'You wanna mix it up, huh?' grunted Floyd. 'You wanna rumble with the big boy? OK, let's see what you got!' He swung murderously at Beethoven, trying to knock him out with a single blow. But Beethoven dodged it and barked loudly.

Floyd took one look at Beethoven's bared teeth and knew that he needed more to defeat the big dog. He snatched up one of the puppies Moe – and waved him at Beethoven, holding him by the scruff of the neck.

'This your kid?' yelled Floyd, jabbing at Beethoven with the club. 'You like this kid? Huh, Pop?'

Beethoven was so angry he could hardly see straight. He jumped forward just as Floyd jumped back, drawing him further and further away from Missy and his children.

'Yeah,' taunted Floyd. 'Come on, dummy.' He waved the puppy in Beethoven's face. 'Come and get junior.'

Quickly, Regina darted in behind Beethoven and snapped the muzzle over Missy's face. The puppies attacked, nipping at her heels and ankles, but she swatted them away.

Floyd continued to jeer, drawing Beethoven further from his family.

'You don't need this many kids. How about if I toss this one off the mountain, Daddy? I mean, you wouldn't miss him!' Floyd dangled Moe out over the edge of the cliff and was about to let him go when he heard a voice.

'Put my puppy down!'

It was George Newton followed by the whole

Newton family. And they were ready to save the day!

But George didn't look heroic to Floyd. 'Back off, Jack,' he sneered. 'You're out of your league.'

'Put the puppy down,' George Newton ordered.

'Yeah? Make me.'

George clenched his teeth and advanced on Floyd. 'I *will* make you!'

Suddenly Alice looked worried. 'George, I'm sure we can talk this whole thing through.'

Mr Newton never took his eyes off Floyd. 'I'm sure we can. As soon as this yahoo puts down our puppy.'

Regina had muzzled and leashed Missy and she dragged her over till they stood behind Floyd. 'Get rid of this drip,' she ordered.

Beethoven could see that he needed to get involved here. After all, it was two humans against one – he needed to enter the battle on George's side.

Just above Beethoven's head, a sturdy sapling grew out of the cliff at a forty-five-degree angle. Lifting his head, Beethoven sank his teeth into the little tree and backed up, bending the sapling like a spring.

'Put down the puppy,' George ordered. 'This doesn't have to get ugly.'

Floyd laughed unpleasantly. 'Ugly? This isn't ugly.' Leaping forward, he jabbed the stick hard into George's stomach, doubling him over, and then smacked him hard on the side of the head, sending him sprawling to the ground.

'Now *that's* ugly,' said Floyd.

At that moment, Beethoven let go of the bent sapling and it snapped forward, whistling as it cut the air. It zoomed over George and hit Floyd flush in the teeth throwing him backwards as if he had been shot!

The stick and Moe flew from Floyd's hands. Ted was off and running the instant he saw Moe soar into the air. Like a big leaguer running for an impossible catch, Ted dashed across the rocky terrain and then dived and caught the little wriggling puppy in his outstretched hands.

The force of the sapling blow had propelled Floyd to the very edge of the cliff, and he tottered there for what seemed like an eternity, his arms windmilling in the air. It was Regina who grabbed him and stopped him falling.

But she failed to realize that she was vulnerable too. No one was paying any attention to Missy, so she edged forward and nudged Regina in the behind and sent her *and* Floyd flying over the edge of the cliff!

Screaming at the top of their lungs, Regina

and Floyd slid bottom first down the steep slope, rocks and tree branches bashing them on the head with every foot they fell. Then, about a hundred feet down, they landed with an enormous splat in a little lake that was filled with black mud as thick as crude oil!

For a moment, they vanished under the dirty scum, then slowly they rose out of the muck, two big blobs of oily dirt.

'You had to hold on to me, didn't you?' snapped Regina. 'You couldn't let go!'

'You mind if I say something?'

'I try not to listen to morons,' said Regina, struggling to get out of the mud.

'Who are you calling a moron!' yelled Floyd.

'Well, I don't see anyone else around here who fits the description quite as well as you do!'

'You know, I've outgrown you,' screamed Regina. 'I really have!'

'Yeah,' yelled Floyd, 'well, maybe this relationship is no longer meeting my emotional needs. You ever think of that?'

Up on the ledge, the family looked down at Regina and Floyd arguing and flailing around in the slime.

'Look,' said George, 'we can't just stand here. We've got to go down there and help them.'

'Aw, Dad,' said Ted, as if George had asked him to take out the rubbish. 'Do we have to?'

'Of course we do,' George replied. 'Even if we don't like them, they're still human beings.'

But no sooner had he spoken those words, than the weak earthen wall on the far end of the mud hole collapsed, sending Regina, Floyd and about two tons of black, stinking mud spilling off the slope and down into the fast-running river in the depths of the valley. The water washed them clean, but it also carried them away screaming, around a bend and out of sight.

And that was the last the Newtons saw of Regina and Floyd!

Chapter 26

Five months later, things had more or less got back to normal. But not one of the Newtons – canine or human – had forgotten the time they spent at Lake MacDonald. And no one in Lake MacDonald had forgotten the Newtons either! Ted and Janie still wrote to each other, as did Seth and Ryce.

In fact, Ryce had got a note from Seth just that day, and she was reading part of the letter out loud to Alice and George.

'. . . "By the way, I'll be coming to town the weekend of December twenty-second to go to the Inmates of Utopia concert. Do you want to go with me? Tell your parents you'll be very safe. Please write soon. I miss you. Seth."' Ryce sighed. 'He misses me.'

'Who are the Inmates of Utopia?' Alice asked.

George had the answer to that one. 'Some savage but socially conscious band that nobody's heard about yet.'

'How did you know?' asked Ryce.

'Aren't they all?'

The doorbell rang and Ryce ran to open it. Standing in the doorway was Mr Brillo, Missy at his side. Her tail wagging, Missy ran over to Beethoven, barking happily.

'She wanted to come and see her kids,' said Mr Brillo. 'I had to bring her.'

Suddenly Ted and Emily ran in from the living-room. 'Our commercial is on! Our commercial is on!'

Ryce grabbed Mr Brillo by the arm and dragged him into the family room. 'Quick – come in.'

By the time George had been ready to make his TV commercial, he didn't have enough money left over to hire actors. So he had used his own family.

Ted and Emily were first up, throwing Newton air fresheners into a dustbin.

'Something's reeking,' they rapped, 'the family's freaking! Throw in a Newton!'

Then Ryce appeared on the screen. 'A serious stench on the exercise bench? Throw in a Newton!'

Now it was George's turn. 'Something offensive? You're hypersensitive!'

The whole family was gathered to watch the commercial – although it was not the first time they had seen it.

'This thing has been on for months,' George told Mr Brillo. 'And it's still bringing in business!'

Suddenly, the puppies got wind of the fact that Mr Brillo was there. They came bounding into the room and pounced on the man, although they were hardly puppies any more. They were huge! Almost as big as Beethoven and Missy!

And where were the proud mother and father? They were outside, running across the lawn, playing and frolicking in the grass. They were so happy, it seemed as if music was playing on the breeze, serenading them as Missy and Beethoven ran into the sunset, together for ever!

SKYLARK
K. M. Peyton

Life isn't much fun for Ben – until he meets Elf and is drawn into an exciting adventure. But the two children must keep their secret from the thoughtless adults in this delightful and touching story.

ADAM'S ARK
Paul Stewart

Oscar's arrival in the house has a dramatic effect on Adam. In discovering that he can think-talk with the cat, he is at last able to make contact with the world around him. But the more he learns about the sad plight of animals everywhere, the more determined he is to discover why he alone has this extraordinary ability to communicate with them.

STORMSEARCH
Robert Westall

It is Tim who finds the model ship buried in the sand and, with growing excitement, he, his sister Tracey and their eccentric Uncle Geoff realize the significance of their discovery. For the model ship yields up a long-forgotten secret and a story of danger and romance.

THE WATER HORSE
Dick King-Smith

Last night's storm has washed up a strange object like a giant mermaid's purse, which Kirstie takes home and puts in the bath. The next day it has hatched into a tiny greeny-grey creature, with a horse's head, a warty skin, four flippers and a crocodile's tail. The adorable baby sea monster soon becomes the family pet – but the trouble is, he just doesn't stop growing!

ESIO TROT
Roald Dahl

Mr Hoppy is in love with Mrs Silver. But Mrs Silver has eyes only for Alfie, her pet tortoise. How can he ever compete with such a rival? He comes up with a bold plan to win his lady's love, involving some clever riddles and a whole army of tortoises. Will Mr Hoppy's patience be rewarded? And what's to become of Alfie?

A highly comic and unusual love story.

JUST FERRET
Gene Kemp

Owen Hardacre, otherwise known as Ferret, has been dragged around the country by his artist father and been to so many schools that he doesn't expect much from Cricklepit Combined School. But when he makes friends with Beany and Minty and gains the respect of Sir, things begin looking up ... even the reading!

Meet Ferret, his friends *and* enemies in this fifth story of the pupils of Cricklepit Combined School.

RT, MARGARET AND THE RATS OF NIMH

Jane Leslie Conly

When Margaret and her brother RT get lost in the forests surrounding Thorn Valley, help comes from an unexpected quarter when the super-rats of NIMH come to their rescue.

Margaret and RT must return home before winter sets in, but the incredible events of their summer in the valley become the biggest secret they have ever had to keep.

The third thrilling story in this classic trilogy about the rats of NIMH.

ONLY MIRANDA

Tessa Krailing

A new town, a tiny flat over the Chinese takeaway, a new school mid-term and a place next to Chrissie Simpson, the most unpopular girl in the class. Things aren't looking great for Miranda. But her father has gone to prison and this at least is a chance of a new life for her and her mother. Miranda bounces back in true style: she befriends poor Chrissie and when the dinner money is stolen and Chrissie is suspected, Miranda is determined to prove her innocence.